SHAMEFUL THRILLS

Girls Who Should Know Better
A Mischief Collection of Erotica

mischief

Mischief
An imprint of HarperCollins*Publishers*
77–85 Fulham Palace Road,
Hammersmith, London W6 8JB

www.mischiefbooks.com

A Paperback Original 2013

First published in Great Britain in ebook format by
HarperCollins*Publishers* 2012

ISBN-13: 9780007534869

Set in Sabon by FMG using Atomic ePublisher from Easypress

Find out more about HarperCollins and the environment at
www.harpercollins.co.uk/green

CONTENTS

Contents

Raising the Stakes
Elizabeth Coldwell

Robin was wrong for me in so many ways. Married, a good twenty years older than me and, most importantly, my father's best friend. The last person I should have ever considered fucking. But from the moment I stepped into the unlocked bathroom on the second floor of his Belgravia home and saw him with his head buried between the bare, spread legs of his children's nanny, it didn't matter that I should have known better. I simply had to have him.

Though I'd only caught a glimpse of his cock, coiled within the tight white briefs which were the only thing he wore, I'd seen enough to know it was big. Bigger, certainly, than anything I'd been used to until then. That night, I lay in bed, nightdress pushed up to my waist and fingers in my pussy, dreaming they were my legs Robin was holding apart with his strong hands, my clit his tongue flickered over till I screamed and came, my cries bouncing off the white-tiled bathroom walls.

I didn't think he'd been aware of my unwitting intrusion. Normally, when you walk in on someone unexpectedly, you make your apologies and leave, but what do you say in those circumstances – 'No, do please carry on, I insist'? What I'd really wanted to do was stay and watch, hoping when he'd reduced the nanny to a panting, satisfied mess, he'd turn his attention to me. Instead, I'd shut the door as quietly as I could and gone in search of an unoccupied bathroom, before returning to the party downstairs, lust and envy seething through my veins.

The next time we were alone, however, Robin made it clear he knew exactly what I'd seen. This was three weeks later, and there'd been a significant change in his household since the night of the party. The nanny had left in a hurry, apparently to return to Edinburgh to nurse her sick mother.

'And with Kirsty gone,' he said, standing a little closer to me than might be socially acceptable as we admired the koi carp circling like ghosts in the pond at the bottom of my parents' garden, 'there's a vacancy in my household.'

'But I thought you'd hired a new nanny?' For someone who prided herself on being smart, having graduated with a first-class degree in English, at times I could be very slow on the uptake.

'You know very well that isn't what I mean, Juliette.' He fixed me with those distinctive eyes of his, washed-out blue with a dark ring round the iris, and a fierce thrill ran through me, centring on my core.

To his credit, he never tried to tell me his wife didn't understand him. I believe she understood him all too well. She knew his tastes, and she had no interest in indulging them. The nanny – and who knew how many other women before her – had performed that function on her behalf. Robin made it very clear he wanted me to be the next. I sometimes wonder if I might have declined his proposition if I'd known then what he actually had in mind. And every time, I know the answer would be no.

'So you'll come over on Friday?' he asked, walking with me back towards the house, casual as though we'd been discussing how profusely Mother's rose bushes were blooming this year. 'Lucy and the kids will be away, and I'm having a couple of friends over for a game of cards. They'd be very interested to meet you.'

'Sure,' I replied, too busy wondering whether his friends were as horny and desirable as Robin to realise how I was sleepwalking into my impending humiliation. 'What do you need me to do?'

'Oh, just top up the drinks, fetch snacks, make sure the guys have everything they want …'

A blackbird sang high in the branches of the silver birch tree, and somewhere in the distance the bells of the local church rang out in celebration of a wedding. Or perhaps they symbolised our unholy union, I thought, smiling to myself as we approached the patio where my father tended his trusty barbecue.

* * *

That Friday, I dressed for my night out with extra care, selecting my prettiest cream lace underwear. The bra thrust my breasts out and up, giving me a tempting cleavage, and the panties had a thong back that left most of my arse cheeks bare. They'd cost me a fortune from a designer lingerie boutique in Soho, but if the sight of me in them didn't give Robin an instant erection, there really was no hope for him. Over those, I wore a dress spotted with black polka dots, its hemline short and flirty, revealing plenty of leg. Just the right combination of innocence and experience, I decided, admiring my reflection in the mirror.

A car I didn't recognise stood outside Robin's house when I arrived, a bright red convertible with the top down. It almost screamed 'midlife crisis', but I was forced to revise my opinion as Robin introduced me to his friends, neither of whom seemed to be the kind of middle-aged loser who needed to supplement his waning virility with an expensive, shiny sports car. Geoff, who had a dental practice on Harley Street, was a classic silver fox, his snowy hair just brushing his collar and his green eyes glittering behind small square glasses with gunmetal grey frames. Michael, who ran a media production company in Docklands, was six foot plus of prime Midwestern beefcake, blond and muscular in all the right places. My pussy creamed just looking at the pair of them.

Introductions made, Robin led us all down to his den. The other two men were clearly familiar with the room, but it was the first time I'd even become aware he had his own basement-level domain, fitted out with everything the discerning forty-something gentleman needed to have a good time. There were a couple of black leather sofas, their cushions butter soft, a full-size pool table, the balls racked up and ready, and a genuine Wurlitzer jukebox. Its multicoloured neon lights flashed as Robin punched a sequence of numbers into it, picking out his favourite soft rock tunes. A bar stood in one corner, stocked with bottles of everything from twelve-year-old Highland malt to vintage champagne. Still believing Robin had asked me over simply to carry out waitressing duties, I took their orders. Scotch on the rocks for Geoff, bourbon and Coke for Michael and a glass of Merlot for Robin. I poured a second glass of the smooth, leathery red wine for myself, and sat quietly sipping at it as the men gathered round the card table.

Robin cut and dealt the cards, explaining they'd be playing poker, classic five-card draw style. Card games bored me, always had, and I wished I'd brought a book to read. However, it soon emerged that Robin had thought of other ways for me to pass the time.

'Juliette, darling, there's a jar of nuts on the bar counter. Could you pour out a couple of bowls for us?'

I hurried to do as he asked, eager to make a good impression on his friends. Filling three small white china bowls to the brim with salted cashews, I sneaked a handful for myself, licking my fingers clean afterwards. Looking up, I saw Michael's eyes fixed on my middle finger as it disappeared into my mouth. Unable to resist teasing him just a little, I sucked provocatively on that digit as I kept eye contact with him, so he couldn't fail to imagine it was his cock sliding between my pink-glossed lips.

Geoff, on the other hand, seemed almost oblivious to my presence – until I placed a bowl of nuts on the table in front of him. Out of view of the others, he ran a hand up my leg, under the hem of my skirt, to cup my bottom. He smiled as he registered how little in the way of fabric covered my soft cheeks. I should have said something, maybe even slapped his hand away – I'd only agreed to serve drinks, after all, not put myself on the menu for these men. But I didn't, because the truth was I liked the feel of his hand there, big and warm, squeezing my almost bare arse with delicious gentleness.

For half an hour or so, I acted the part of the dutiful waitress, fetching more drinks, more nibbles, as and when the men requested them. Geoff grew bolder in his moves; the next time I lingered in his orbit, his hand closed round my panty-clad crotch, gently pushing the soft lace up into my cleft, causing my juices to flow strongly. I bit my lip, trying to conceal my reaction to his fingering, but a tiny squeak of pleasure escaped. Robin looked at me, his expression seeming to strip me bare. I didn't know it, but with the acknowledgement that I was enjoying everything his friend was doing to me, I'd given him permission to put the dirty little scenario which was to be the real meat of the evening into action.

I hadn't been following their poker game at all, but Michael appeared to be the dealer at this point. Robin was studying his cards intently, doing his best to keep his facial expression neutral as he weighed up his options. Geoff had already folded, throwing his hand face down on the table, though it seemed, from the size of the pile of chips in front of him, he'd been doing considerably better than his friends up to this point.

At last, Robin tossed a couple of chips on to the pile in the centre of the table. 'And I'll raise you five pounds.'

Michael matched the bet, and waited for Robin to decide what he was going to do. His options seemed limited, seeing that he was already down to his last chip. He threw it on to the pile, his next words taking me completely by surprise. 'And I'll throw in Juliette's dress, too.'

It was an outrageous offer, but I reckoned he had to be pretty confident in the cards he held to make such a deal. And anyway, there was no way Michael would accept it – or so I thought, until he smirked and said, 'OK, I'll see you.'

Robin spread his hand out on the table, face up. Michael, his smirk now so wide it threatened to engulf his entire face, did the same. If I'd known anything at all about poker, I'd have been aware there was no way Robin's random selection of cards could have beaten the array of queens and aces Michael revealed, and understood just what kind of game he was actually playing. But I remained in ignorance, even as Michael said, 'Looks like I win. Pay up, sweetheart.'

With a shock, I realised he was addressing me. Holding out a hand, he drawled, 'Let's have that pretty dress of yours.'

This couldn't be happening. Robin couldn't have gambled away the clothes on my back, surely? But all three men were looking at me expectantly. It seemed a bet was a bet, and I had no option but to unzip the dress. I peeled it down off my shoulders, stepped out of it and handed it over to Michael.

'Thank you so much, Juliette.' His tone was gracious, and I thought that was the end of my ordeal, but then he smiled and said, 'Get me another bourbon and Coke, would you, darlin'?'

Blushing furiously, I went round to his side of the table and picked up his empty glass. When I turned and walked to the bar, I knew all three men would have a perfect view of my bare arse, cheeks bisected by the scandalously small thong back of my panties. The only thing for it was to try to back away, treating them to my front view only. Though that in itself was quite a sight, with my big brown nipples pushing at the cups of my bra, and the telltale spot of dampness in my panties from where Geoff had played with me.

Michael just shook his head, and I knew my plan had been rumbled. I turned round and dashed to the bar, wondering just why, if it was so shameful to be running about half-naked in front of three men almost twice my age, my pussy was fluttering with excitement and my nipples were quite so hard.

Returning with his drink, I saw the cards were being dealt again. Despite having been cleaned out by the last hand, Robin was still in the game. Maybe his friends had agreed to take an IOU in lieu of cash, I thought naively. It wasn't as though he didn't have the money to cover his losses; the expensive boys' toys on display in his den were evidence enough of that.

This time it was Michael who folded, Geoff who faced Robin down in this contest of bluff and counter-bluff.

'So what are you willing to stake this time?' Geoff asked, in the tone of a man who knows he's literally holding all the cards. 'Your Rolex? That bottle of 1982 Margaux I know you've got squirreled away in your wine cellar?'

'In your dreams, Geoffrey.' Robin sipped his Merlot. 'How does Juliette's bra sound?'

I should have realised this was coming. Neither of Robin's friends appeared at all surprised by the offer, and I wondered how many times in the past they'd brought Kirsty the nanny, or some other willing woman, down here to take part in their perverse gambling games. Geoff merely put his cards down on the table with a wolfish grin. 'I'll see you,' he announced.

Even before Robin's hand was revealed, I knew he'd lost. Three pairs of eager, greedy eyes turned towards me. My protests that I couldn't possibly do this were half-hearted, hands already reaching behind my back to unfasten the catch of my bra. Still, I strung the moment of my exposure out as long as I could, clutching the cups to my breasts while I eased the straps down off my shoulders, so as not to show them everything straight away.

Geoff held out an expectant hand, and I pressed the bra into it, still doing my best to cover my bare tits with one arm.

'Now, now, Juliette,' Robin chided me. 'Show my guests what they've come to see.'

I could only describe the feeling that overcame me on

hearing his order as one of pure submission. Being made to display myself to these virtual strangers had woken something in me I'd never known existed. Letting my arm drop to my side, I stood and allowed them to take in the sight of me topless, nipples tight knots of desire.

Geoff put the bra to his cheek, enjoying its silky softness, breathing in the perfume clinging to it. 'Exquisite,' he murmured. I wasn't sure whether he referred to the underwear, or me.

'What do you figure, boys?' Michael asked. 'One last hand, winner takes all?'

Robin nodded. I didn't have to be a rocket scientist to know what he'd be throwing into the pot. As nervously excited as I'd ever been, I watched as the cards were dealt, the bets placed, my panties staked against two piles of chips. As he looked at his cards, something in Robin's body language changed, though I'd no idea whether the other two were aware of it. Maybe they were too busy dreaming of the moment I would have to present my disgracefully wet, fragrant underwear to the winner. Call it feminine intuition, but I knew Robin had a winning hand. Until now, he'd been deliberately playing to lose, contriving to strip me naked for the delectation of his friends in the process. Would the cards he held affect his strategy, and change the course of the evening?

'I'll see you,' Michael said, Geoff having folded with a rueful shake of his head.

Robin laid out his cards. Three kings and two fives. 'Full house.'

Geoff, at least, was impressed, but the smile on Robin's face faded as Michael counted out his own cards in sequence. Ace, king, queen, jack and ten. All hearts. 'Royal flush. Sorry, Robin, you lose.'

I couldn't help thinking Robin didn't look as disappointed as he might, had they been playing for serious money. He just sat back, and waited for me to give Michael his winnings.

Again, I took as long as I possibly could easing out of my panties, legs tight together so they only got the merest flash of my secret places. That morning, dreaming of all the wonderfully filthy things Robin and I would do when he finally got me alone, I'd trimmed the hair on my mound into a cute heart shape. It had never occurred to me when I reached for the razor that the sight might not be for his eyes only.

Keeping one hand over my pussy, trying to preserve some scrap of my modesty, I passed my panties to Michael. Just as Geoff had done with my bra, he put them to his nose and breathed in, inhaling my scent as though to imprint it on his memory for all time.

'Darlin', you're truly beautiful,' he told me, 'but the way you're standing, I just can't get the answer to the question that's been bothering me all night. You see, I'm really keen to know if you're a natural blonde ...'

The implication was obvious. A flush rising to my cheeks, I took my hand away from my pussy. Michael's gaze seemed to penetrate between my legs as though it was laser guided, seeking out my hidden treasures. In response, I simply grew wetter, turned on beyond belief. I'd never been completely naked in front of three fully dressed men before, and though I felt so vulnerable and ashamed at how easily I'd been persuaded to undress for them, my body burned with uncontrollable desire.

They must have known in that moment I would do whatever they wanted me to, needing the feel of their hands on my body, their cocks in my mouth, my cunt, wherever they chose. Robin, though, seemed determined to make me wait for that pleasure.

At that moment, the selection of tunes he'd programmed into the jukebox came to an end, replaced by a tense, anticipatory silence.

'Would anyone like to hear more music, or shall I ask Juliette to unplug the jukebox for the night?'

The general clamour seemed to be for the latter, and when I glanced over at the jukebox I realised why. With the socket low down on the skirting board, I'd have to get down on all fours to pull the plug. In that position, I'd be giving them a perfect view of the wet pouch of my pussy from behind. Any thought of objecting disappeared when they rose as one from their chairs, revealing trouser crotches straining at the seams.

I dropped to my knees and crawled over to the wall, knowing perfectly well their eyes would be glued to my bare arse and the dark cleft between it. Someone groaned, and I thought I heard the grating sound of a zip coming down, but I didn't look over my shoulder to see whose excitement had got the better of him. After flicking off the switch, shutting the jukebox down, I waited for my next instruction.

Instead, I felt hands gripping my bum cheeks from behind, kneading and flexing them. 'So fuckin' gorgeous.' The American-accented tones let me know it was Michael who groped me. He'd won the poker game and now he was claiming the real prize of the evening: the chance to be the first of the three to fuck me.

There was so much I didn't know about this man, I thought, as his hand burrowed deep between my thighs. Was he married? If so, did his wife turn a blind eye to his indiscretions, in the same way Robin's appeared to? At that point, none of it mattered. 'Where do you want me?' was all I asked, feeling two of his fingers sliding up into my cunt and a third probing at the entrance to my arse.

Michael guided me over to the sofa, positioning me over one of the arms so my backside jutted out, cunt primed and ready for him. He didn't waste any time, just extracted his cock from his jeans and pushed into me with one long, easy thrust. I cried out at the sweetness of the penetration, finally getting what I'd craved from the moment my panties had finally come off.

As he fucked me with fast, jabbing strokes, Robin and Geoff came close, stroking their own erections as they waited for their turn. I couldn't help noticing that Robin's dick was every bit as big as I'd suspected when I'd taken the sneaky peek in his bathroom that had set this whole perverse chain of events in motion. Even though Michael was warming me up so beautifully, I'd really feel the thickness of it stretching my walls apart.

My tits bounced with every stroke, and my clit was a hard bead of sensation, responding to the stimulation of my own rapidly rubbing fingers. I tried to let my audience know how good this sustained fucking felt and how much I needed to have them inside me, too, but my words came out as garbled moans. Michael stepped up the pace, thrusts growing more erratic, and I knew he was on the verge of coming. He pulled out of my cunt, and I looked back over my shoulder to see him give his cock a couple of furious tugs before his spunk shot out to decorate the small of my back in pearly strings.

As he stepped back, spent and grinning with satisfaction, Geoff rushed to take his place. The skilled hands that more usually gripped dental tools smoothed over the curves of my hips and arse, and I expected to feel the fat head of his cock sliding up where Michael's had so recently been. Instead, he gave my bum an affectionate slap before moving round to my head. When he pushed his cock between my lips, encouraging me to suck, I felt the first sweet spasms of orgasm gripping me. But my passion peaked at the moment Robin entered my pussy with a series of short, assured thrusts.

As he slid home, packing me to the hilt with his hot sturdy length, I experienced for the first time the thrill of being full at both ends. I gripped the arm of the sofa.

'Thank you, Juliette,' he murmured, 'for being everything I'd hoped you'd be – and more.'

I'd had no idea when I'd rung his doorbell earlier that my evening would turn out like this, with a cock plugging away relentlessly in my cunt while I licked and slurped on another. And with Michael stripping out of his clothes and slipping something onto his dick that I knew to be a cock ring, designed to keep his reviving erection hard for as long as he needed, the fun wasn't over, not by a long way.

Together, these three men had introduced me to the pleasure of humiliation, teaching me there was honour in shame and fulfilment in submission. And with these boys-only evenings a regular fixture in their diaries, I could only wonder what other delightfully deviant experiences might be on the cards for me in future.

The Auction
Janine Ashbless

She should have been able to see the stars. They were deep in the wastelands and it was late night by the time they came to put her up on stage, so the stars must have been beautiful. But the compound lights were so fierce that when she was dragged out by the two men and looked round, blinking, all she could see were the lights themselves, the crowd and a glimpse of the chain link fences beyond. Fires burned in old oil drums and their smoke made the light hazy. No stars, no desert hills, no escape.

The crowd whooped and roared. Someone sounded an air horn from the top of a beat-up Humvee.

'Well,' said the auctioneer, coming forwards to take her from her handlers. 'Let's get a look at our next lot, shall we?'

All evening she'd watched the other prisoners being taken up out of the display pen, one by one. Between lots there had been pounding music, whipping the crowd up. She was almost the last to go.

'We've got ourselves a pretty little copperhead here,' the auctioneer said, taking her elbow and steering her to the front of the stage. His other hand held a sweating beer bottle just as casually. He was a lanky man with a shaved head and tattoos that crawled over every bulge of his muscled arms, and he was miked up so that he didn't have to raise his voice to be heard. 'Looks shy, doesn't she?'

The crowd bayed and jeered.

She dipped her head, her long hair falling over her face. She couldn't hide it any other way because her elbows were joined by a twist of rope behind her back, leaving her hands free but tethered helplessly low. The tautness of the rope forced her to arch her back and thrust out her tits and ass – just as they wanted.

'First time on the block,' said the auctioneer, grinning. His skin gleamed with sweat. 'Can you see that blush? She's practically a virgin.'

She squirmed with shame as the catcalls and whistles rose to a new crescendo. She was wearing only tiny cut-off jeans and a deep-necked T-shirt hacked off so short that it barely covered her breasts. There were big manga-style boots on her feet but they didn't make her feel any less vulnerable, only clumsy and uncertain of her footing, like a newborn calf. Above the boots, hold-up stockings covered her to mid-thigh. They had been white to start with, but now they were stained with dust, and the lace was torn.

'What do we call you, Red?' he asked.

'Antonia.' The word seemed to burn on her lips.

'Sweet. You scared, Antonia?'

'Please ...'

'You should be.'

Her legs nearly gave way under her and only his grip on her elbow kept her on her feet. The shift of her hips made the tight shorts press into her ass crack and she gasped with discomfort, but the sound was masked by the gales of laughter from their audience.

'D'you know what's going to happen to you?'

She shook her head.

'Of course you do. I'm going to sell you to the highest bidder, bitch.' The insult was savoured, and Antonia felt the heat run through her body like a shock wave. 'Whoever wants your cunt the most tonight is going to get it. Of course, you'll be lucky if he only wants your cunt – and not every other orifice. See anyone out there you like the look of, Antonia?'

She twisted her face away, shutting her eyes, but he transferred his grip to the nape of her neck and squeezed warningly.

19

'Look at them. You're here because you're worth money to them. Look them in the eye – it's the last chance you'll get.'

She looked. There were – what? – maybe a couple of hundred people out there, men and women, standing near the front or sitting on the hoods of cars and lolling across parked motorbikes further back. Black clothing and leather predominated, where they had bothered to cover up against the night air. It looked like a scene from a *Mad Max* movie. There were a lot of grins, but not one of them reassuring.

'One of those lucky people is going to be fucking you real soon. One of them's going to own you, bitch. You know what that means? They can have *anything* they want from you.'

Antonia couldn't help whimpering. She was shaking with tension and she knew he could feel it.

'Shall we have a look at the goods then?' he called out, and they answered with enthusiasm. 'Right.' He parked the beer bottle between his belt buckle and his stomach – where it stuck up like a crude glass erection – and tugged a small piece of plastic from his pocket. It was a cable tie. Scooping up the smooth fall of coppery hair that Antonia was so proud of, he twisted it into a rope and secured it with the tie. His movements were swift and practised. 'I like to see a good handgrip on a slave,' he informed her, wrapping the bright ponytail around his left fist and pulling her head up and back. Tears brimmed in Antonia's eyes.

'Now, I see we've got a good big pair of tits on this one,' he remarked to the crowd. He retrieved his bottle, took one last sip and then upended it over her breasts, dowsing both thoroughly. Shame burned through her body all the way to her core. The liquid was chilled and the smell of cheap beer made her head swim. She was aware of the sudden pull of her nipples as they tightened in response to the unexpected cold shower, poking out against the taut and now clinging cloth.

The auctioneer tossed the empty bottle back over his shoulder. She heard it smash.

'Yeah, that's nice,' he purred, flicking her nipples with his nail to accentuate their jut and pinning her as she flinched. 'Imagine getting your cock between these, gentlemen. Look at the size of them! And real too! But don't take my word for it; see for yourselves.'

He pulled something else out of his back pocket and held it up for Antonia and everyone else to see: a knife handle. Its blade flicked out, glinting gold in the compound lights. She gasped, but he took no notice. Holding her firmly, he slipped the knife up between her breasts, caught the point of the T-shirt's V–neck and pulled. She felt the jerk of the cloth across her shoulders and neck, but the blade must have been very sharp because the cotton gave way almost instantly, splitting down the front to let her breasts spill out. After putting his knife away, the auctioneer cupped one orb and jiggled it.

'Now, we don't see many like that nowadays, do we? The genuine article. Heh. For the real connoisseur.' He slapped her breast to make it bounce, then took hold of the nipple and pulled it up and out, hefting the weight. 'And not pierced – yet. Well, buy her and ring her.'

He wrenched the shredded shirt off her back and turned her this way and that along the front of the stage to demonstrate to everyone the quiver and bounce of her flesh. The beer gleamed stickily on her bare skin and her nipples pointed at the crowd as if trying in vain to pinpoint an ally. Antonia could feel herself pulsating with shame. She knew her mascara was leaking down her cheeks already.

'Nice figure too, I think you'll agree, ladies and gentlemen. A beautiful big ass. I'm betting that'll soak up plenty of punishment.' To demonstrate, he clapped his palm loud and hard against the swell of her bum cheek and Antonia let loose an inadvertent squeal of shock.

The burn seemed to swell even as the pain died away.

'Oh, a little sensitive are you, darling? That'll be fun.' He winked at the audience. 'And a good pair of lungs on her, I hope you notice. Mind, she'll need to be able to breathe through her ears, given what one of you horny

22

fuckers will probably be doing to her before the end of the night.'

'Please,' she begged, 'please let me go! I shouldn't be here, I need to go home –'

'Shush.' His fingers were oddly gentle as he pressed them to her lips, cutting off her protests. 'No one's listening. Nobody cares.' Two of his fingers slid into her mouth. They tasted of iron and oil and sweat, and Antonia worked frantically to accommodate them and not gag as he pushed them over her tongue, right to the back of her mouth. 'That's better,' he sighed. 'You're beginning to get it, aren't you?'

As he withdrew his fingers his attention snapped back to the crowd. 'Of course, ladies and gentlemen,' he announced, snuggling up to her rear, 'what you really want to see is her pussy, isn't it?' With the word 'pussy' his voice dropped an octave and the mic vibrated. He was playing up to the theatre of it all, and she was doubly sure he was enjoying it because, through his abraded jeans, his hard cock was jabbing gleefully up against her.

'Yes!' shouted the crowd – and wilder, more obscene things too.

'I don't blame you.' The auctioneer's spit-wet fingers trailed over her chin and down her throat and between her breasts. 'You don't buy a car without looking under the hood, do you? And you don't buy a fuck-slave without getting a good look at her pussy.' He smoothed his hand down the slight curve of her belly and insinuated his fingers beneath the waistband of her cut-offs. His thumb flicked open her fly button with a casual expertise. 'Want to see?' he teased.

'Yes!'

'Turn around,' he ordered, spinning her to face the back of the stage. 'Now, be a good little bitch and bend over.'

Antonia had never anticipated this. She could feel the sweat of her panic gather at the small of her back. It hardly felt real: the blood was pounding in her ears and her head was swimming. But the stage was backed by big polished steel panels, allowing her a blurred and distorted view of what was going on behind her: the crowd, the big man controlling her every move. She was not to be allowed to forget that she was being displayed and sold in public.

'Bend,' he growled, planting a hand between her bare shoulders to tip her from the hips. She tried to comply, awkward because her arms were tied and she couldn't brace herself with her hands. She almost lost her balance and he grabbed the back of her shorts to steady her, sending a lightning stab through her private torment. Her fingers dug fearfully into her hips. He kicked her feet further apart. Her ass and tits were now stuck out in perfect counterbalance.

The knife came out again to dissect her cut-off shorts.

She felt its cold steel whisper against her skin. It gave even the stitched denim short shrift, and after a series of agonising yanks the garment fell away down her thighs, revealing to the world her ass and crack and the shy peek of her pussy below.

That was the first moment of relief Antonia had felt since coming on stage.

'Whoa,' said the auctioneer, appreciatively. 'What have we got here, ladies and gentlemen? It looks like there's been some customisation going on with this one.' He put a hand between her cheeks, prodding the rubber bung that jutted out there. 'I don't know if you can see this clearly, but she's got a big black butt-plug up her already.'

His fingertips explored her stretched anus, discovering the thick greasy lubricant that they'd filled her ass with before inserting the plug. Antonia hadn't tried to fight when, an hour before her entrance on stage, they'd held her down and worked the dildo into her – she had been too afraid of the hefty cylinder now riding her ass. The discomfort and the sense of imminent disaster and the humiliation had been almost overwhelming, and those tight shorts had only made the sensations worse, every step a torment.

Now it was the auctioneer's turn. He jiggled the dildo inside her and made her wail.

'Well, look at that, ladies and gentlemen. She's lubed up and stretched and wide open. I think that when you buy her, you're going to be able to just whip that butt-plug out and stick your dick right in there to fuck that beautiful ass, like going into warm butter. So I'm going to leave it where it is for the moment.'

He chuckled. 'Told you it's always worth taking a close look before you buy. Now, let's examine this pussy.' His hand cupped her sex. 'Well, if you can't see, you can take my word for it. This one's nicely shaved, every bit of her. Soft as a kitten, this pussy.' He bent and both sets of fingers explored her sex, not at all rough – but thorough. 'She's got rings, ladies and gentlemen. I count three on either side, outer labia, silver. Someone's taken a lot of care with this one. Fucking beautiful example, and I see a lot of them in this line of work. And –' his fingers spread her '– she's running wet. Jeez – that is one juicy fucking cunt! I don't think you'll have any problem warming this one up. She's just begging to be taken out for a ride!'

Antonia sobbed, mascara tears running down her cheeks. Her pussy seemed to throb under the merciless glare of the auction lights. But the examination was not yet over. He slid his licked fingers into her passage and spread them. With the internal pressure of the plug in her other hole, it was enough to make her squeak.

'Mmm. That's good. Tight enough to give you a good firm grip, I think. And ...'

She felt the fingers withdraw again. She saw in the

26

blurred reflection how he straightened up and lifted his hand to his face.

'Sweet. Tastes like honey, ladies and gentlemen. I think we've got a prime piece of cunt here.' Tugging her pony-tail, he slapped her ass and jerked her upright. 'There's one last thing, though. Want to see how she performs?'

Of course they did.

He brushed his lips to her ear. 'Get on your knees.' He didn't push her, but his voice was like the black oil from an engine sump and she was incapable of diso-beying. Her legs seemed to fold of themselves and she came to rest on the rough boards of the stage, her head on a level with his crotch. She watched as he unbuckled the big worn belt around his hips, tugged down his fly and manhandled out an uncut cock that was already fighting for its freedom. Like the rest of him it was long and sinewy and lumpy with veins.

The calls of the crowd had become white noise. She felt the muscles of her asshole clench around the cruel plug between her cheeks. She could smell the harsh mascu-line sweat of his groin.

'Lick it, bitch,' he crooned.

She hesitated, cringing from that unfamiliar cock.

'Fucking lick it.'

This time she moved in and licked him tentatively, from root to crown. His flesh was hot and his glans was sticky. Her tongue slithered over the dome of flesh and

27

she tasted his musk with something like dread. She thought she'd done enough to satisfy him – but without warning his fingers stung her cheek in a slap and then, as she gasped in shock, he took advantage of her parted lips to push her mouth down firmly over his bell-end.

'A slave shouldn't need to be told twice,' he growled, angling his cock and her head so that he could plunge all the way to the back of her mouth. As he filled her throat, Antonia swallowed hard, desperate not to gag on his length. Grinding his hips, he bedded his meat firmly in her. He held her there a long time, almost until her air had run out, while the crowd voiced their appreciation. Then he pulled out slowly, revelling in the glistening trails of saliva and the rush of her breath and the heave of her breasts.

'Well,' he said, tucking his erection nonchalantly away and pulling her round to face the crowd once more. He stood behind and above her as she knelt there panting, his hand tight in her hair to ensure that her face was visible, his legs straddling her flanks, his sheathed cock rubbing up against the back of her head. 'I think we've seen all that we need to. A nice little specimen. Let's get this sale started. I'll set the bids off at $50 – do I have any takers?'

At that price there were plenty of takers. The bidding went in a rush and the price spiralled. But by the time it got to $800 there were only three bidders left. Antonia, blinking, focused on those faces. Her fate depended on who won this contest, and fear made her chest tight. One bidding group was a trio of three young men, all egging each other on. One was a couple sitting astride a parked Harley, both in leathers. One was a lone man, a face she recognised, and her gaze met his in terror.

He'd watched her in the display pen. He'd had eyes for none of the other lots, as far as she remembered: he'd just watched her with that same scowl that he sported now. No matter how many other people had drifted back and forth, ogling the flesh on offer, laughing or admiring or sneering, he'd always been there in the background. She'd been kneeling, her wrists roped to a peg driven into the dirt, her thighs spread either side of it. She'd looked up from under her lashes and watched him sliding his blunt fingers slowly up and down the erection outlined by his leather pants. He wore cowboy boots and an open leather waistcoat that showed the sandy hair furred across his belly and chest. His jaw was square, his hair cropped, his expression as hard as the bulge of his cock. That expression, the uncompromising harshness of it, had made her heart run fast and weak. It was as if his face epitomised the brutal greed of the crowd and the hopelessness of her captivity. She'd looked at him and known there would be no mercy.

Not that her other prospective purchasers promised any more kindness. She focused on the couple on the bike. Both were middle-aged. Her hair was peroxide blonde, his in a grey ponytail that matched his beard. There was a chrome ring through his septum, as if he were a bull. He had a whip looped at his belt and she – leaning forward to whisper into his ear – carried a riding quirt stuffed down her capacious cleavage, behind her shiny PVC corset. Antonia could only imagine how they would take turns to use those whips on her tender flesh, and she quivered with fear. She could feel her sweat trickling down her ass crack into her pussy, as if in anticipation of the pain.

But then the biker couple dropped out of the bidding.

She switched her focus to the trio, though her hearing was becoming distorted and her eyes were blurring with tears. They looked sort of normal, though they were shirtless tonight. Regular enough guys apart from a slightly exaggerated muscularity: quite young, no obvious piercings. They shared the same tattoo on their right shoulders, and she guessed from its shape that it was a military crest and that they were army. Or ex-army. But *three of them* – would she be able to cope?

Would they take her one at a time, or would they get what they could all at once?

She couldn't help picturing what that might entail and she shut her eyes as if that might block out her imaginings, only to see them painted in brighter colours in her mind's eye. Her mouth was dry with tension and she ran her tongue round the inside of her lips, trying to gather some moisture.

Then suddenly the bidding was all over and she opened her eyes to see the three men shaking their heads in disgust and gesturing dismissively. She'd been so caught up in her own sensations that she'd actually missed what the winning bid was, but she could tell that the lone man in the leathers must have won. He was striding towards the stage now. The military trio jeered and that sentiment was taken up by the crowd, a rolling wave of amused disparagement.

'Up,' grunted the auctioneer, pulling her to her feet.

It was cash only, up front and no waiting around, at this sale. The man in leather handed over a wad of bills, and the moment he'd counted them the auctioneer pushed Antonia down the steps into the hands of her new keeper. 'Congratulations,' he said with a leer.

Close to, the pores of her purchaser's leathers were highlighted with dust. He smelled sun-baked, with a dash of bourbon.

If she'd entertained any last hopes that he would be gentler than the auctioneer, they were rudely dashed then. He gripped her rope of copper hair and pulled her head back so that she was nearly tipped off balance. Her ass tightened painfully around the plug. Then he pushed her before him through the reluctantly parting audience so fast that she stumbled and caught her feet. He didn't

31

seem to care that she was bumping into people and her breasts were slapping against the arms and chests of grinning bystanders. He took her straight to the back of the crowd to where the cars were parked, and there planted his rear on the hood of a 1950s Ford. 'Knees,' he said, shoving her to the floor between his feet.

She couldn't understand why he was being so rough or why he sounded so angry, when there was no resistance left in her. Tears welled up in her eyes as she looked up at him through the crazy shadows. From this angle he was only a black silhouette against a blazing compound light.

'I noticed you seem to like the taste of a strange dick.'

That was so unfair. What choice had she had? 'Please, you don't have to ...'

'Shut up.' He yanked down his zipper, his haste undisguised. His cock was big and ruddy and smooth-looking, and its slitted mouth was already weeping with eagerness.

Antonia took a deep breath and opened her mouth obediently to accept it.

'No. Kiss it.'

She blinked.

'Kiss it, you dirty slut. I paid a shitload of money to have you, and you belong to this dick from now on. It owns you. Whatever it wants, you give it. Whatever it likes doing, you like too. In fact you *love* it. So kiss the cock, fuck-slave.'

He angled his erection to her lips and she kissed it, mouth to mouth, tasting his pre-come with the tip of her tongue. A kiss seals a pact: it comes with a signature, it vows obedience. The softly pursed rose of her lips met his flesh in token of her submission.

'Fuck yes,' he murmured. Then he dragged her up by the hair and dropped her face-down on to the hood of his auto. Antonia caught a glimpse, in passing, of a silent semicircle of watchers: clearly some of the crowd had followed them back here to see how it would pan out. Her breasts squashed against the warm metal and her feet scrambled for solid purchase on the desert ground. A big rough hand cupped her sex to haul her rump up.

'Spread them,' he ordered, and slapped her upthrust ass hard, once on each cheek. Stiff-legged and with her arms trapped at her sides, she could only obey. She didn't have time to even catch her breath before his cock seared into her sex, slippery in her juices but pressed tight against the mass of the plug in her other hole.

She cried out.

'Good 'n' tight,' he grunted.

He started to thrust, settling into long smooth powerful strokes that made no allowance for the rubbery length already occupying her and constricting the space available. His hand on her hair did not let go – in fact it tightened, stretching her throat and forcing her back to arch. With every thrust, the wall of his belly prodded the butt-plug deeper into her, and she felt like she was being impaled from her ass all the way up her spine and out the top of her head. Her clit was grinding against the car's hood ornament. She could feel herself falling apart.

'What are you?' he snarled in her ear, his spit spraying through his teeth with his effort.

'Your slave!' She could no longer see anything of the real world: light and dark flashed in her field of vision.

'Yes – my slave – my hole – my piece of ass. Sold, bought, paid for. Mine. Now and for ever.' The pounding was a terrible thing and she was disintegrating beneath it with every blow. 'Now tell me how much you fucking love it!'

She broke out in a shriek, as he hammered her orgasm into her like it was a nine-inch nail. And as her last incoherent cries died away he pulled out, took a grip on the evil nub protruding from her ass and drew the butt-plug out from her clenching and dilating anus. She heard the wet sound it made as the seal with the lube broke. For a moment she was empty – emptier than she had been in her whole life, it felt like – and then he filled her all over again, driving his hot hard meat deep into her rear passage to shoot his load inside her.

Antonia was still in the grip of her orgasm and these new thrusts lifted her up and threw her over the top again into a second climax. As he pumped his seed into her, she felt her ass open like a desert rose under his bitter rain.

She was still sobbing with release when he laid his hand on her back and stroked down her spine, gentling her as he stooped and nuzzled his lips to her cheek.

'Toni ... You OK there?'

'Yes. Jesus. Fucking *yes*.' Her aftershocks ripped out of her as a peal of giggling hiccups. She knew she was making no sense. Her mind felt like a puddle sloshing wildly round inside her head. 'Ray. That was ... Oh, *fuck*!'

* * *

They were sitting contentedly together with a group of people watching a rather beautiful blonde get the words 'cum-slut' tattooed across her shaven mound, when the auctioneer found them.

'Toni. Ray.' He bumped knuckles with Ray's lazily proffered fist, but his attention was on her. 'Was that all right, Toni?'

'It was amazing, Jonas,' she said warmly, leaning into Ray and rubbing her cheek against his bare shoulder. 'It was ... intense! And you were great.'

His grin lit up his face. 'Glad to hear it.'

'Although,' said Ray, 'I don't actually remember telling you it was OK to stick your dick in my wife's mouth.'

Jonas shrugged. 'Hey. Improvisation.'

Toni giggled. She'd been finding it hard not to for the last half-hour: she was still buzzing on the endorphins. 'It worked for me.'

Ray brushed her cheek with his knuckles. 'Hey, you were so into the zone ...'

'Damn right,' said Jonas. 'That was a fine show. You're something special, Toni.' He pulled out a sheaf of papers and held out one to Ray. 'This is your receipt, by the way.'

'Receipt?'

'For your kind donation to the club's annual fundraiser.'

'Our pleasure.'

'And next year ...' He crooked an eyebrow at Toni. 'How about somebody else getting a chance to buy you, for real this time?'

'Maybe,' she said, grinning. The thought sent a warm pulse through her sex. Somebody else purchasing her for the night? Perhaps somebody she didn't know? Maybe more than one of them? She gave her hips a little squirm, enjoying the tingle of trepidation and arousal, and looked up at her husband, wondering if he realised how much the thought excited her.

'Maybe,' growled Ray. 'We'll see.'

Touched
Ashley Hind

I cannot touch her because she is too flawless and beautiful. To do so would painfully reignite the embers of my still glowing desire. Just the slightest contact could rekindle the burning torment of all my days, the empty agony of my unrequited love. I cannot touch her because she isn't even quite half my age – not just young enough to be my daughter but also in reality my own daughter's best friend. Not just my daughter's best friend but eldest daughter of *my* best friend, Veronica, the closest ally and most cherished companion I could ever wish for. Roni and I have been inseparable since before I can even remember, and I have loved her, hopelessly and with slavish devotion, for all of those years.

Therefore I cannot touch her. No matter that she is

even prettier than her mother, whom I have always considered the most beautiful person alive. She shares all Roni's best features. She has the same liquid brightness of her dark-chocolate eyes, the thin jet-black punctuating lines of her nostrils and eyebrows against the pale skin, the little comma dimples high on both cheeks and the grey-shadow faintness of another at her chin. But her nose is smaller and ever so slightly upturned. Her smile is wider and more radiant. Her movements are quicker and more captivating. Her hair should be dark but is instead golden blonde, and her overall demeanour seems somehow softer and more accessible. She loves to laugh and to tease, retaining the sassiness of her youth while blossoming through her teens with the confidence and maturity that seem to bless the most perfect of our species. She lights up every room she enters, and must set every heart within on fire – it cannot surely just be mine.

My blood has only ever pulsed this hard for Roni. My fingers only ever drained cold and tingled like this for her. I thought she would be the only one to make my breath stick in my lungs, and I feel treacherous now for the involuntary reaction of my own body. I cannot recall a time when Roni was not as integral to me as my own organs. We were almost like Siamese twins in our youngest days and growing together through puberty. It was always assumed that she was the dominant partner, the one who made our decisions and shaped our lives. I never sought to contest this. Outside of 'us' I think I had influence and was never regarded as her puppet. I think most of our peers held us in equal awe, dislike or indifference, depending on their individual whims. I have been told that I am pretty too, and perhaps I am, but I always felt that my looks were immaterial other than in how *she* perceived them. I guess I could have been stronger, but being besotted with someone strips away your will and power base, and so she became my personal Fate, the one who decided my actions. I just stayed at her side, praying day on day that she would love me the way I loved her.

She knew and enjoyed the fact that I yearned for her. My adoration was written in my innate regard for her welfare even above my own, and in my helplessly doe-eyed gaze. Sometimes this would elicit a cuddle from her, and she would say *ahhh* as she rubbed and patted my back for comfort. She was never mean to me or used my adulation for her own ends. She just took it for granted that if she wanted to do something then we should do it together, and I never once contradicted this. Although my feelings towards her were obvious, I never declared them or tried to bring a physical element to our relationship. In fact it was her decree, coming out of the blue during one of our countless sleepovers, that we should 'practise kissing' to help cope with the onslaught of boyfriends that she envisaged for us around the next corner.

I can still remember the heart-stopping softness of her lips that first time. She could feel me tremble and sigh and she broke off to touch her forehead to mine and whisper, 'Come on, sweetie – this is only to practise, remember?'

When I nodded my acceptance she kissed me again, and let me melt into her. Our lips stayed locked together for over an hour that night, our tongues eagerly exploring as our hands chastely stroked each other's arms and back. I revealed nothing that might spoil the chance of a repeat performance of this most exhilarating episode. I never told her how wet it had made me, more so than when I lay alone at night and split the folds of my virgin pussy with a single delving finger, and squeezed the protective cloak around my little clit in an attempt to suppress the throb that persisted there whenever I thought of her, which was all of the time.

Despite countless opportunities she made me wait maybe half a year before she deemed more 'kissy practice' was necessary, and thereafter the lessons we took together were sporadic and always at her suggestion. Although our snogging bouts were wet and animated, her hands always stayed at my sides or back, her swirling tongue a direct contrast to her almost imperceptible caresses. She allowed me some greater boldness, letting me stroke and even squeeze her soft bottom through the cotton of her pyjamas. One time, she even let me cup her small tits and, to my undying delight, she exhaled a little sigh and I felt her nipples harden beneath the fabric. But whenever I got carried away, squeezing too amorously or attempting to slide my hands inside her protective nightclothes and on to bare skin, she would pull out of the kiss and touch her forefinger to my nose or mouth, always giggling the same phrase: 'Not just yet, you naughty lezzer!'

It was a playful chide that was supposed to be in jest but still defined the difference between us.

With this added contact between us, my need for her became harder to contain, but was still never vocalised, although she could hardly have been in any doubt that I wanted her beyond words. After one night of kissing, when she thought I was asleep, she reached out with tentative fingers and felt the dampness that had soaked the crotch of my pyjamas – proof, if any were needed, of my aching desire to have her completely. And so my love for her was as clear as the Ionian waters that we swam in on the day she finally allowed me to make her come. It was our first holiday abroad together, one that she had picked and arranged, and one that she had decided would herald our full introduction into adulthood. It was our chance, she said, to release our inhibitions and enjoy the freedom of life. It was a chance to do whatever we wanted to do.

I was barely able to do anything. The sight of her all

day long in a skimpy bikini and her skin shining with lotion seemed to dissolve my insides and have them flowing embarrassingly into my own bikini bottoms. I was forced to don sparsely protecting sarongs and either lie steadfastly face down, or sit in scrunched, cross-legged ridiculousness on the sunbed. The heat only made it worse, inflaming my passions and my nipples and addling my brain so that I could barely think straight or form sentences. In the end she noted the near-paralysis of my desperation and she took pity on me. In the swelter of the afternoon, with me incapable of speaking more than single words and my stare fixed upon her beauty, she raised her eyes and tutted, and smiled as she gently shook her head from side to side. Then she took me by the hand and led me back to our apartment.

'Kiss me,' she said. 'Not for practice this time, but because I want you to.'

In most of my dreams our lovemaking was slow and gentle, but our one and only fuck proved to be anything but. Our skin was slippery with sweat and sun oil and our clothes slid from us with ease as my hands wandered with free rein all over her body, and she reciprocated at long last. Her passion wasn't forced and was as urgent as my own. She grabbed my bare arse then slapped it three, four times before crushing the pliant flesh between her fingers once more, all the time pulling me in to squash and rub our soft, hot mounds together. We knew how to kiss each other, that's for sure – but this time my usual avidness was matched by hers, and we wetted each other's cheeks and chin in our hunger. We slithered together in the heat of it, using any and every part of each other's body as we saw fit. We covered each other in trails of our juices, in our sweat and saliva. If I had known then that it would be the last time then I would never have washed again – but it seemed to me then like it was just the beginning.

'You know,' I said, 'that I will never want anyone as much as you, however long I live?'

She smiled and nodded and kissed me again. How could I possibly have known that I was wrong? She lay back and raised her legs in the air and stretched them apart so that I could bury into her sweet puss and feel it spread against my face. With her sun oil she smelled and tasted like coconut milk, and I drank her down thirstily. I could have made her come with my tongue alone, but I wanted the first time to be mind-blowing. I slid two fingers inside her and stirred them in wide circles, feeling her unctuous juices ooze down on to my palm. Then I fucked her with swift in-and-out pumps that had my hand slapping loud and lewd against her bouncy, sopping slit. The gentle stroking of my fantasies had evaporated in my lust.

The sound of her slurping pussy was beautiful, but it was eclipsed by the sighs, squeals and gasps she emitted as she came, her whole body tensed rigid and arched off the bed, her inner muscles clenching my fingers as if they never wanted to let them go. It took ages for her to come down from her climax, and I wore each second with ever growing pride. When she was finally able to speak, she took me by the hair and splayed me out on the saturated bed.

'Your turn now,' she said.

We fucked for hours, the years of pent-up desire bursting through and our holes too slippery and willing to deny any invasion. My pussy flowed unabated throughout (even today on the odd occasions she makes reference to my pussy, she stills calls it my 'little gusher'). My slick juice covered us both unremittingly, until she cried out, as the heat and exhaustion slowed us in our tracks, that I would drown her if I did not stop. I wanted to stay awake all night, to lie by her side and just gaze at her and bask in my delight, but sleep took hold and, when I awoke, she was already preparing to go out to eat.

The thought that we were now lovers was quickly quashed. Roni announced that it was now time for boys, and over the next couple of days she set about lining up suitable candidates. I floundered at her side, too heart-broken to offer resistance and consumed with the need to get into her bed again. Somehow, at the very end of our holiday, she contrived to have us facing each other across the kitchen of our apartment, her with one leg up on a chair and me leaning across the breakfast table, whilst two local barmen pumped us from the rear and lost us both our virginity.

The whole incident remains something of a blur, and no doubt alcohol plays a big part in this. I remember being too dry. It gave me a dull ache and little pleasure. I remember that I was topless with my skirt up over my back and my knickers around my thighs. Roni's man had stripped her from the waist down but had not bothered with her top in his haste to get inside her. My pumping partner was completely forgotten and I was absorbed in them alone. Her man was unshaven and rough-looking, and his jaw jutted out as he grimaced with his array of sex faces.

I can't remember his name but it may as well have been 'Dagger' for all the hurt he caused me with each piercing thrust up into my beautiful Roni's perfect body. I hated him. I could see his white-knuckle grip on her, and the impossible thickness of the purple-brown base of his cock. The rest of his shaft was pinked by his condom and shining with both lubricant and her excitement, sliding out of her then slamming back inside as he held her steady. She was eyes-closed and trembling, loving each centimetre of penetration he was giving her, and that I never could. I remember her eyes coming open and fixing on me as she set into the long rise of her climax. She wanted to see me, to share this moment when we lost our innocence for good, to witness my enjoyment too. Through her breathless gasps she said, 'I love your big tits,' and then she readied herself for her orgasm.

All I could do was rub myself like crazy and try to time my release with hers. I just about managed it, and we closed our eyes on the scene and took our separate pleasures, hers loudly, mine in defeated silence. My man was not as well prepared as hers. I tersely told him he couldn't come inside me, so he came around to seek solace from my mouth, and was in turn refused this also. With barely disguised contempt he tossed himself off over my face and called me a bitch. That I do remember.

Having experienced a cock for the first time it was all that Roni could think about. I knew I'd lost her, even if I couldn't admit it to myself. I was swept up and taken along for the ride. Back home she soon fell for Steve, so I was obliged to go out with his best friend (I shouldn't complain overly – he was and is a kind and gentle soul, a doting father, and he has perhaps more claim to feel wronged in all of this than me). As unprepared as ever, I managed to fall pregnant within a year, at about the same time that Roni announced that she and Steve were to get engaged. Then the idea bloomed and before I knew it a double wedding was planned and executed, my dress stretched over my bump and my daughter kicking inside me as I was led down the aisle. As I stood side by side with my Roni at the altar, she beamed and told me that she was pregnant too.

* * *

I've never blamed her for all this and I was overjoyed that it kept us close. Our daughters grew up together, as close as we two ever were. The older they got, the more we could see us in them. We began to spot the crush forming and the potential heartbreak building, although we never discussed it. The girls were left to their own devices, history left to repeat itself. Perhaps part of me wanted my daughter to succeed and conquer where I had not, to let me borrow some of her joy at having the most perfect person to call your own. Part of me simmered with jealousy though, and the girls' shared closeness was a bitter reminder of what I had never achieved.

I loved my husband the best way I could, but I always loved Roni more. I couldn't help it. She was inside me, vital to my body and soul. He knew this too. He knew I would have loved him more if I could but I just wasn't built that way. We finally separated, very amicably, three years ago. Roni is still with Steve and they have two other children. We see each other almost every day, but my aching desire to be in her presence is finally diminishing. Our daughters remain inseparable. They are as close to us as they are to each other. Even so I still didn't see it coming.

Roni's daughter has the look of love in her eyes but I didn't spot it until it was too late. I should have seen it when she used to come around and chat even when she knew I was alone, or when her lips inched closer to mine each time she took her goodbye kiss. I should have realised as soon as she started to compliment me on how I looked. I should have taken her aside and nipped it in the bud that day she told me that she loved my big tits and said she wished that hers were like mine. I should never have started to wear low-cut tops for the first time in years in the hope of catching her attention. But if you are in your late thirties as I am, you don't expect to be doted on by younger women, especially ones so lusciously sexy. I could have avoided flirting with her but it just shot me through with excitement. I didn't have to smirk and jiggle my chest at her whenever she caught my eye and surreptitiously mouthed the words 'Big tits!' in my direction. I should never have let her sneak her chance to come up to me that one night while my daughter was out of the room. I could see the mischief in her eyes and in her smile but I didn't know how to stop her. I should have tried to fend her off before she got so close she was able to make me shiver with a tongue-tip trace on my neck, and the hot breath in my ear as she quietly said, 'I want to fuck the arse off you.'

Of course I told her *no*.

'A thousand times no,' I said. 'There is too much between us to possibly make this right. I can see in my daughter's eyes that she loves you and it would pull her inside out if you chose another. It would rip her to pieces and I would know every inch of her pain.'

All of this I said to her, as clear as day in my head. But when my mouth was finally able to form the words, when they stumbled out all breathless and whispered and shaking, all they sounded like was: 'Oh God – yes!'

They slept together that night, as they always did and always had done whenever she stayed over. I couldn't sleep for thoughts of them together, hope and jealousy all rolled into one. For my daughter to have found love with one so perfect should have been everything to me. For tortured hours I lay awake, picturing them together and praying that they *were* actually lovers, knowing full well the agony if they were not. I then had to quickly push the images from my mind once the bitterness of my solitude shrank my stomach and sickened me. Eventually I found myself crawling on my hands and knees down the hall towards their room, trying not to creak the floorboards, trying to hear any evidence of their passion, desperate to know one way or the other. I heard nothing from their room and, although my shame rushed through me, all I could feel was elation. I was on all fours and wretched in the darkness, my frantic fingers breaking the silence with sticky slurps from my desperate puss as I imagined the girl creeping down the corridor and slipping into my bed. To have been caught in this moment would have been beyond any conceivable ignominy, but still I wished she would secretly open the door and find me on my knees before her, and deliver me from my raging frustration. She never did come that night, even when I did, audibly panting on the floor outside their room.

So you see that I am already lost in her and that's why I cannot touch her. For the sake of my sanity, for the sake of my friendship and my daughter and everything I hold dear, I cannot touch her. But above all I cannot touch her for the simple reason that she has bound my hands behind my back with duct tape and I am physically incapable of doing so. She has pulled my tits from my blouse and pinched my nipples hard. She has thrown my skirt up and cut my knickers free with scissors and plunged her fingers inside me to make my little gusher flow. She has wiped my juice all over my bum cheeks and hungrily licked it off. Now she is parading in front of me, her head cocked to one side and the smile spread across her beautiful face. Her white shirt is undone and her perky little tits are bare and peeking out. Her tiny grey pleated skirt is raised up and draped over the huge black dildo protruding from her waist. She is gently wanking the toy up and down its length, smoothing a lubricating oil into its surface.

I can feel her behind me now, touching my thighs and bum, stroking at my slit to wipe the juices all around. The dildo is at my tight entrance, pushing forwards, sliding on my slickness and opening me up, driving forwards and stretching me like nothing else, making me cry for joy as it fills me. She is fucking me now, holding my bound wrists and slapping the dildo in and out of me. It feels huge, like I am a virgin again, like this is my very first time. Only this time I know I will never forget a single detail. My thighs are soaked and my bum is wobbling and slapping and I feel like the orgasm is going to explode and burst me apart. I am yelling and it is coursing through my whole body, wave after wave. My legs are shaking and the lights are flashing in front of my screwed-shut eyes.

I am still panting but I can acknowledge the relief of the tape being severed at my wrists to free my hands. She has come around in front of me while she unstraps the dildo. I can see it thickly covered in my come. Her skirt has come off now and she is gently rubbing her clitty in small circles and pulling up the flesh to expose the little bud beneath. I know she wants me to suck her.

'My turn now,' she says.

If I keep my hands to myself I cannot grab her soft bottom and pull her in. If I don't reach out I cannot expose her aching clit and give her the pleasure she craves from me. If I touch her now there is no going back. I could lose the love of my life and will almost certainly see my own daughter heartbroken and crushed. Or worse, I might be used this once and then left to suffer another lifetime of the nightmare of placing my passion and soul at the door of someone who cannot, *will not*, love me back. But my hand is already reaching forwards. Although I am burning with anxiety and treachery and guilt, still I see it inching out slowly to pull her to me and make her mine, and I really don't know if I have it in me now to make it stop.

Watercolours
Primula Bond

I know I'm supposed to be setting a good example, but I'm starting to regret this. I can't feel my extremities any more. The slightest movement in the room kicks up dust. I can see specks of it floating in the weak daylight. It tickles my nostrils, but I can't even sneeze.

There's rain, sliding down the big north-facing window. Across the narrow street there's a warehouse-type building like this one. I can see blurred figures over there, talking on phones, glaring at computer screens, stretching and yawning in dreary meetings. I can just make out one bored bloke staring out of the window, like me, at the wet world.

Amazing how thick a silence can be even with a dozen people clustered together. One person clears their throat every so often. Someone else shuffles their foot rhythmically under their chair. Apart from that the only sound is the wisp of wet brushes stroking paper, and the footsteps of Stuart marching importantly about behind the semicircle of easels.

'How are you doing, Caro?' he calls over. 'Like a break?'

I daren't move or speak.

'I must say I'm enjoying this role reversal,' he laughs. The other students laugh with him. Christ, he's really taken over, hasn't he? 'And I'm *really* enjoying the view! She's sexy out of her overalls, isn't she, guys?'

The guys all murmur their agreement, and swish their paintbrushes even more vigorously.

'You could wink, or something, to let me know if you're tired,' he says.

I moan, but it sounds pre-orgasmic.

The students put down their brushes and flex their arms exaggeratedly into the air. Across the street a strip light flickers on. The afternoon is becoming night.

'I'm turning to stone here.' My voice is scratchy and my neck creaks when I try to turn it. 'Can we stop?'

Suddenly the studio is empty and I'm left alone. Even Stuart has dashed off. All mouth and no trousers, that one. Chickened out of being on his own with me because I'm naked. Pity. He's quite cute. I don't normally go for beards, but his is more of an overgrown stubble and he's wearing an old fisherman's sweater the same sky blue as his eyes. He has long legs, clad in ripped jeans ...

Tut, tut, Caro. You should know better.

I'm stiff, and freezing, and I've only myself to blame, because it was my idea, when the life model didn't show, to take her place.

'We need some curves, anyway,' I reasoned, as we set up for the session. 'You know, big breasts, hips in the right places, none of your skinny nonsense.'

'Go for it, Caro,' Stuart, late as usual, growled in my ear. 'We'll even pay you!'

I'm quite proud of my body, though it's been months since I undressed it for anyone, let alone a load of art students. And I'm a bit more Rubenesque since I last had a lover.

Nobody moved, so Stuart marched me across the dusty wooden floor of the attic studio.

'Clothes off.'

I tried to look composed as Stuart sat me down on a box covered in a rich purple fabric and started to manipulate me into the correct position. His hands were strong and warm on my spine.

Stuart's really a sculptor, and his fingertips are roughened by all that chiselling. They pinched at my chin and bumped over my ribs. He seemed to be moulding me like a clay figure. My flesh started to tingle as his callused skin caught on each tiny hair, but his fingertips didn't linger.

He raised one arm, and my breasts bounced up and down with my rapid breathing. Even sitting there in public, feeling shy with all those people watching, his touch was making me horny.

'Honestly, Caro, looks like you'd be turned on by a handshake!'

I glanced at Stuart's crotch, to see if he was aroused. I couldn't see any bulge. He tugged me about with the detachment of a surgeon, crossing my feet, pushing my dressing gown off one shoulder so that he could balance a polystyrene urn there, and arranging my hair so that the curly ends brushed my exposed nipples.

I tried to catch his eye. He fussed with each strand, hooking my hair carefully round the darkening points. Surely he was taking longer than necessary, or did it feel like that because I was tense with embarrassment? Sure enough the edge of his thumb knocked against one taut bud, and both nipples sprang into action, the burning points standing out red against my pale skin. I caught my breath with a stab of excitement but that only had the effect of lifting my torso and thrusting my tits out further.

One or two of the students shifted in their chairs and I smiled to myself. That's right. I was back in control.

Stuart dragged the gown right off so that cold air caressed me. He frowned, then started pointing at the various parts of my anatomy the students should be concentrating on. While he talked and while they kept their eyes on anything but the rigid points jutting out at them, I struggled with the mad urge to leap across the room and start lap dancing round their easels.

'Just relax, Caro,' Stuart said at last, stepping away to the back of the room.

That was hours ago. I get up now, stiff as an old lady. So much for being in control. But I need to cover myself. I feel unreal, like one of Stuart's statues. It's as if my skin is whiter from being exposed, my bones crystallised from keeping so still. My eyes are dry with staring into space.

I wrap the purple brocade round me, and totter to the window. The man on the other side of the street has gone.

'I wanted to catch you,' someone says. I jump. I thought everyone had gone. Now I see that there's one easel that hasn't been packed away and someone is reflected in the glass pane, hovering behind me.

'I've finished for the day,' I say, too tired to turn round. 'The next life class is tomorrow morning, I think.'

'I can't wait until tomorrow morning.'

It doesn't *sound* like Stuart. A draught from the ill-fitting window skims over me, making my skin shiver. The lights in the office across the street go out.

'Why can't you wait?' I ask.

'I need to paint you tonight. I've this project, you see, has to be presented first thing tomorrow morning, and you are perfect. I wondered –'

'No way. Sorry.' I sigh, pulling the wrap tighter. 'I can't sit for another minute. I've cramp in my arm from holding that bloody urn up, my bum's numb, my neck won't twist, and I have to get down to the cashier's office before they close.'

'I've got wine. And the budget will cover it – I mean, I'll pay you.'

I hear the chink of glasses. Now that's a sound that never fails. I swivel round. He has his back to me. I don't recognise the pinstriped trousers and the creased white business shirt, but then again I've been in such a trance all afternoon that I wouldn't know any of the students if they jumped me in the street.

'It's tempting.' I lick my lips as he pulls the cork. 'But I'm knackered. I just want to lie down, close my eyes –'

'You can do that. No more uncomfortable poses, no more urns to hold. I'll do all the work. You don't have to lift a finger.'

'Well, I suppose I could spare a few minutes,' I say slowly. 'If you tell me your name.'

'I'm Antony. Now, come over here.'

He goes behind a Chinese screen in the corner of the room where I've accumulated a velvet chaise longue piled with cushions, a palm with leaves quivering in the breeze and an old standard lamp, which Antony switches on to cast a soft glow. The rest of the studio is in darkness.

The set-up looks so welcoming that I can't help it. I

fall backwards into the nest of cushions, aware that the brocade wrap is slipping off me. My limbs loosen sensuously as the softness closes round. My legs are splayed apart, one on either side of a huge purple pillow, and my arms are flung above my head.

'You're a natural,' he says, tweaking the brocade away. It slides over my breast and my nipples harden again. A swathe of velvet drapes across my pussy in a mockery of modesty. 'That's just how I want you. All classical, and vulnerable.'

He pours out the wine and hands me a glass. I sit up to swallow deeply, and see him properly for the first time.

'You don't look like an art student,' I say, putting the glass on the floor and lying back again. 'Why are you wearing a tie?'

'We don't have time for questions. You're in a hurry, and so am I. Now close your eyes. Are you happy like that?'

His face swims as I lose focus. He is running his tongue over his lower lip. His voice is so quiet that I think I'm already asleep. The rain has started up again outside.

A leaf from the palm starts tickling my foot. I flick my foot away lazily, but it must have blown in the breeze because now it's brushing up and down my skin. I think of those servants who used to cool their ladyships in India with huge fans. Were those fans made out of palm leaves? But it's cool enough in here already. The palm leaf has reached my knee now, and the sweeping movement is stronger. The leaf feels heavier now. It also feels wet.

When it moves still further up my leg and alters its course to caress the inside of my thigh, I open my eyes.

Antony is kneeling over me, delicately holding a paintbrush. A sliver of gold paint gathers at the sable point, elongates, and drips to the floor. He crouches sideways, not seeing me watching, and dips the brush into a big pot. A golden line snakes its way up my leg, winding round the upper thigh and into the fragrant shadows under the brocade.

'What are you doing?' I ask softly. He looks up, his tongue trapped between his teeth like a small boy's. Now I can see his eyes. They are brown and fathomless under a shock of brown curls, but they are twinkling. I grin, and kick my legs so that the brocade nearly falls off.

'Painting you,' he says, holding his reloaded brush up. 'I told you. Painting you all over.'

'What's this project, then? Creating some sort of Cleopatra figure?'

He just laughs, and traces another line up my other leg. My flesh quivers beneath the slight pressure, yearning for his paintbrush to press harder, and to press higher. Already my legs look like they belong to someone else. I keep them spread as he wanted them, heavy as lead, but underneath the fragment of brocade my pussy is moistening.

'You'll look like some sort of gilded animal when I've finished with you.' A gleam ignites in his dilated pupils but he looks away to dip the brush again.

'Let's hope you never finish with me, then,' I say, my voice harsh with sudden desire. The paint is thick and wet on my skin. Each stroke feels like a tongue licking me, but as the paint dries it starts to crackle and sparkle, and itches like hell. It's going to be a ferocious act of will to remain still while he paints me, but it's all in the cause of art, isn't it?

Antony rolls his sleeves up and loosens his tie before designing some fancy curlicues around each of my ankles. I sigh loudly and fidget a little on the cushions. Something hard digs into my backside and wedges up between my cheeks. I rock as subtly as I can, keeping it fretting against me, a foreign body rubbing round from my tight butt hole towards my damp fanny. I gasp and bite my lip as it slides between them, opening the secret crack a little and scraping like a shock against my clit.

As my cunt starts to throb my instinct is to give it something to suck. I want to cram something inside, but the object slides through my bush and the tip emerges from under the brocade. I stifle a giggle. It's another paintbrush, long and elegant, the bristles clean and soft.

I lift it and twirl it between my fingers, and the sable

catches between my breasts. I push them together with my arms, trapping the brush there, then pick it out and dust the bristles in circles over each full breast, round and round the aching nipples, teasing myself mercilessly, hitching myself further down the couch so that I can abandon myself more fully to the pleasure.

Antony is still hunched over my leg, but his brush is spent and resting against my knee. I push past him, nearly knocking him over where he kneels. I dip my own brush into the pot, and bring it back up to my breasts clumsily so that gold paint drips all over the brocade and leaves shining globs on my stomach.

'Oh, what a mess,' I say, smearing the brush from my navel straight up to my throat and back again, circling my breasts so that now the animal's torso is striped with gold and my brush needs replenishing. 'We must be careful of this lovely wrap.'

I lift the brocade and Antony snatches it sideways. A whisper of air creeps underneath and I wriggle with the cold. His golden artwork stops just short of my bush.

'That doesn't look right,' he mutters, plunging his brush into the gold paint and waving it above me. 'We're running out of time.'

'So finish the job,' I say, pointing my brush like a spear. He bends down and runs the brush in quick strokes up both legs so that the design meets over the triangle of curls. I look like an exotic zebra. We both gaze at my new jungle beauty, and another jolt of excitement shakes me because I can see he's transfixed. I lift up one knee, not bothering to ask him if I may. The whole design is altered now. There is the unmistakable wet slurp of pussy lips parting. He hears it too.

Still grasping the paintbrush, Antony bends lower as if he wants to sniff me. My skin prickles eagerly. The tip of his tongue wets his mouth, then flicks out across my puss. Instantly I hook my knee round his neck. He aims his tongue more carefully a second time, slicking it up the hidden slit, flickering from one plump lip to the other so that sharp sensations start to sizzle through me. My involuntary groan clangs in the empty studio.

We both freeze as a sound carries through the building, perhaps triggered by my loud groans. It could be footsteps on the stairs. I have no idea what the time is. I don't care. Antony seems to have forgotten the urgency of his project too.

After a moment of listening, he grabs my buttocks and lifts my hips right off the couch and then at last he buries his face right into the tight curls, nipping the tender area with his teeth, pausing as I quiver, and then licking rapidly, lapping at my sticky cunt, pausing, then making me shriek as he sucks on my burning clit, sucking so hard that my body is already straining to find a peak of sensation.

His tongue flicks mercilessly through my pussy and

then I realise his other fingers are crawling between my buttocks, moving and sliding inside, tickling and pushing, then suddenly at least one finger enters my tight little ass hole which puckers and grips around his fingertip. There's a delicious sliding sensation in my belly as his finger creeps further in. My body sucks at it, and then he starts to thrust it in hard, pulling out, then joining forces with another long finger to make a thicker tool and together the fingers impale me.

Against my leg I can feel his groin moving with the same rhythm as his head, and the hard shape of his cock is rubbing against the bone of my shin. I can't get hold of him to fondle him. All I can do is arch myself up, rocking on his fingers, offer my sex to his greedy mouth and enjoy the spasms of pleasure knotting together in that special spot behind my navel.

All the while I get to work with my paintbrush, sweeping it wildly over my tits, tickling and caressing my nipples with the bristles so that they send their own hot shafts of excitement down to join what Antony's mouth and fingers are doing. I start to writhe and grind myself into his face and he gets the message because now he's lapping fast like a dog as the spasms arrow themselves from all parts of me, my cunt, my backside, my tits. I start to buck, afraid I might break his teeth or nose, too bad, can't help it, cushions soft on my back, air cold around us.

I quiver and moan, tangling his hair around my fingers. I toss my head about on the cushions while he holds still, tongue pushing and lapping, fingers poking and penetrating, and then I find my strength and pull his head away from me. I want the real thing, now, and I bet he does. My pussy twitches frantically as his warm mouth comes away. He unzips his trousers, kicking them away. There's a clatter as he knocks the paint pot over, but he can't stop now. The lid spins on the hard floor like a top. There's his cock, jabbing impatiently at the inside of my leg so that it, too, gets decorated with blobs of gold.

I toss my paintbrush to one side and open my arms to him. My tits are swollen with excitement, the nipples hard as acorns, and I thrust them towards him as he crawls on top of me and stares down at my gold-spattered body. The paint must be oozing across the floor.

'What will Stuart say?' I murmur.

My juices are still shining on Antony's lips and chin, but his cock is jumping now, the shaft highlighted with squiggles of gold. I wipe the swollen knob end, and already it is beading with spunk. I wrap my legs once more around his slim hips and pull him into me. His tie dangles in my face. I take the end of it, tickling it across my nipples. He smiles. Just as his stiff cock meets my wet cunt, his wet mouth meets my throbbing tits and I wonder if I can hold on for even a second as he rams it up inside me at the same time as taking one nipple in his teeth and biting hard.

Now I really do scream out loud, gripping him between my knees, flinging my arms back over the couch, arching with my spine to milk every tiny sensation out of this. My limbs are fluid and strong. I can't imagine ever sitting still again.

My whole body is pushed up the couch with Antony's energetic humping, and then he makes one almighty thrust and we fall off the couch on to the floor, into the pool of gold, which splashes and sticks to us. I am gripping him like a limpet, and now my hair is all wet, but all I care about is the shaft of muscle filling me and pumping at me. Antony lets my nipple spring free and pants wildly, staring at me with those dark eyes, and I realise he's close, and I let it all go.

I cling on to him. He tries to lift me back on to the couch, but I'm heavy. His knees and hands slip about in the paint and we fall back into it. Every time he moves, droplets of paint find a new surface of skin or clothes or hair to gild, but nothing will stop us now. He gives up, rolls with me, then we hump and bump on the floor and at last the arrows of pleasure zooming about inside me hit their target, sensation gathering, building, and at last exploding. His cock hardens inside me, then he spurts his load and I shout and laugh with delight that my body has come alive once again.

Antony rears up over me. His white shirt, tie and even his trousers are smeared with gold paint. The paint has spread all over me so that my legs are almost completely painted now instead of decorated with elegant stripes.

'I look like the girl in *Goldfinger.*' I start to laugh as he swipes his hand uselessly at all the stains. 'Is this how your project was supposed to look? Or was that just a trick to come and fuck me?'

'Certainly not a trick, though the fucking was a bonus,' he says quite seriously, packing his cock away in his gold trousers. 'I genuinely do have to present something to my bosses in the morning. And now we're going to have to start all over again. The painting, I mean.'

'Can't you just leave me to dry?' I'm still on the floor, just as he left me.

He ponders. Even the curls of his hair are tipped with gold. 'Good idea. But stay exactly as you are. I have to get my camera from across the road.'

'Across the road?'

He looks like an Oscar statue. 'I saw you from my office window, earlier on. Those luscious curves and bare breasts picked out by that halogen spotlight. Perfect. In fact I thought you were a sculpture at first, which gave me my first brainwave. So I ran over here, asked the tutor if I could run amok with my pot of paint, and discovered you were a real live, extremely horny woman.'

'He's not the tutor –'

'And that's why I got carried away, I'm afraid. But now you're back to being a statue.'

I try to move, but once again my limbs feel like lead. The paint has turned into a kind of glue. My arms are stuck where I flung them happily above my head. My legs are wide open, splayed like a rag doll, my bush dusted with the drying paint. My nipples really are golden nuggets, now. My hair fans out, turning into wavy twigs of gold.

'For God's sake, what *is* the project, Antony? And like I said, he's not the –'

'Hi, Stuart! Didn't see you there! God, this is so going to get me a promotion!' Antony is shaking transparent liquid out of a bottle and dabbing at the stains on his trousers to clean them. 'We're going to plaster her on billboards all over town. She'll be Cleopatra. Spreadeagled, just like that, on the studio floor, in a puddle of gold. She'll be the muse for our new campaign to promote this industrial gilt paint. Normally it's used on picture frames, furniture, railings, even gates and door knockers.'

'Grand,' drawls Stuart, somewhere in the room.

The only muscles I can move are my eyes. Even the specks of dust dancing in the air look like golden showers. He's seen me fucking this bloke from across the street. I squeal, 'Let me go!'

'Oh, Caro, you should have known better,' Stuart laughs quietly.

'Just got to get that photograph!' Antony calls, running down the stairs. 'Then she's all yours, Stuart.'

'But, Antony,' I croak, as the studio door bangs shut, '*I'm* the fucking tutor!'

Great White Arcs
Jennie Treverton

Aimless Amy felt her nickname was undeserved. Friends mocked her for her lack of ambition but Amy thought they'd overlooked those few instances in her life when she'd come across something she actually wanted. It was a rare occurrence, but when it happened she was quietly unstoppable.

Take the recent office reorganisation, a lottery for even the most senior staff of Stellar Engineering, let alone a lowly HR assistant like Amy. With a strategy of flattery and reverse psychology she'd managed to get her desk positioned near the back wall, facing the door, buying her a vital few seconds in which to minimise her browser whenever the boss walked in.

Life was good for Amy. She had MSN Messenger and

an oblong patch of sunshine on fine afternoons. One morning she was browsing for shoes when in the edge of her vision she saw the CEO, Andrew Petterly, approaching.

'You're awfully busy, Amy, aren't you?' he said. 'We won't keep you long. I want to introduce you to our new head of innovation.'

Amy clicked her mouse, sat back and smiled. She liked Andrew, and he liked her because he drank in the same pub as her father and shared with him a passion for quizzes and cricket. Andrew was a notorious figure in the civil engineering world thanks to his invention, in the late 70s, of a new traffic management system inspired by the form of the female breast. The legend went that shortly after the birth of their first child Andrew had watched his wife Stella expressing breast milk and realised that he was looking at one of the most efficient flow control methods devised by nature. He studied the internal structure of the human mammary and saw, in the intricate branchwork of capillaries and ducts, an idealised city plan where traffic could be pulled through by what he called 'stroking' and ejected from the urban centre via a concentrated number of superhighways. He was only a junior assistant at the time and had to convince the senior partners of his firm. So the story went, he took Stella along to help him demonstrate his method. Before the panel of executives he bared her breasts and manually stimulated her until she spurted great arcs of milk across the boardroom table.

At least five major towns across the UK were based on Stella's tits.

'Charles, Amy is our HR dynamo,' said Andrew, patting the top of her screen with affection as if it were her shoulder.

'Charlie,' said the man next to him.

'Charlie. Pardon me.'

The first thing Amy noticed about him was his tongue. In the weeks to come she'd muse on that fact. After all, there was nothing particularly unusual about it, except that it was beautiful. Quite flat, delicately rounded, a rich pink.

'You want my details then,' Charlie said to Amy.

'She'll leave no stone unturned, this one,' said Andrew.

Andrew started to tell Amy about the new position he'd created especially for Charlie, who interjected here and there with self-deprecating comments that made Andrew laugh, and Amy kept looking for glimpses of Charlie's tongue. She noticed that he was dividing his eye contact absolutely equally between her and Andrew. Big brown eyes and an effortlessly polite manner that had obviously charmed Andrew's socks off. He was tall and well-built, about thirty, with a cleft chin and wheat-blond hair that brushed his eyebrows. He had a wide face with prominent cheekbones. Last of all Amy noticed the platinum wedding ring and her stomach hit the floor.

Having never before been in this position, Amy wasn't sure if there were any circumstances under which it would be deemed harmless fun to flirt with a married man. What if she did it quietly and subtly? Or loudly and ironically?

As the weeks went by she tried different tactics and slowly a common rhythm developed, based on banter and innuendo and light ridiculing of Andrew Petterly. They'd happen to meet at the water cooler or they'd happen to leave the office at the same time. He showed her his motorbike that she'd feigned an interest in. She volunteered admin support for some of his projects.

In the boardroom one day she was helping him prepare for a meeting. They weren't talking, just getting on with the job. He went to find extra chairs. She set out water and glasses and his voice came up behind her. 'I bet you shave your cunt.'

Amy shivered. A thousand thoughts ran through her head. 'How can you tell?' she said, turning to face him, sliding her butt on to the table.

'I just can. What shape do you do it? Or do you take the whole lot off?' His gaze was even.

'Well, it depends,' she said slowly. 'If I'm in the mood, I'll shave it bare. But usually I leave a little triangle at the top, like an arrow.'

'I see.'

'It looks really nice,' she said.

73

His expression was remote. He could have been asking if she'd remembered to polish the glasses. 'So,' he said. 'Have you got one of those clits that pokes out all the time?'

'I can see you're building up a mental image here,' she said, laughing.

'Do you?' he said, not laughing.

She met his eyes and saw nothing she recognised. Her smile faded. Finally, she shrugged and said, 'I don't, actually. It only comes out on special occasions.'

His gaze drifted as if his thoughts were elsewhere. Then he left the room without a backwards glance.

In fact the only housekeeping Amy did on her bush was a quick trim with the scissors whenever the edges got too wild. She went home that afternoon and shaved it thoroughly, saving a triangle at the top.

A few days later she met him on the stairwell. He stopped a few stairs below her. His gaze began at her shoes and rose unhurriedly to the hem of her skirt.

Enough is enough, she thought. Aimless Amy took aim.

'It just occurred to me, Charlie. You haven't taken me on that bike ride yet.'

'Oh, OK. When do you want to go?' he said.

'Well, the bank holiday's coming up. Most of us are taking half day Friday. So, how about Friday?'

'If you like,' he said. 'You got a helmet?'

'No.'

'I'll bring you one.'

If you like. So casual she wanted to kill him. And when Friday came he wasn't in the office. Casually, Amy asked around but nobody knew where he was and she couldn't dig any deeper in case she raised suspicion. All morning she kept an eye trained through the window on the car park. She sent calls through to the wrong people and slammed her thumb in the drawer of the filing cabinet. At three minutes to one she turned off her computer and looked outside. No Charlie. Full of disappointment, she put her coat on and left.

She walked into the sunlight and her heart bounced like a rubber ball to see Charlie on his bike, his gloved hands drumming the tank impatiently as though he'd been there ages. He had a fat orange sports bike and a helmet covered in chaotic lightning. His leather jacket was tight across his broad back. As she approached he produced another helmet for her, a white one. It was too small to be his.

His wife's, thought Amy.

She straddled the pillion awkwardly, wondering whether to grab the bar behind her or hold his waist. She wasn't sure what the done thing was, having never sat on a motorbike before. She'd never been so close to him before, either, and suddenly her thighs were around him and her pussy pressed against his arse. The machine simmered beneath them.

He's married, she thought.

It felt totally wrong.

She put her arms round his waist and clung on tight as they shot away. 'Where are we going?' she shouted.

He said something she couldn't make out. She decided she didn't care. Soon they were on the motorway and then they were on winding country roads, flying past fields and reservoirs.

He slowed and shouted over his shoulder, 'I don't have much time. Only an hour.'

'Oh, no, really?' she said, disappointment welling again.

'We're going to London. Debs booked tickets for a show.'

Amy rolled her eyes and let go of his waist.

'Do you want to stop for a cup of tea?' he said.

What she wanted to say was, *No, I fucking well don't want tea*.

'Sounds good,' she said.

They entered some woodland and Charlie veered into a lay-by shielded from the main road by trees. There was a burger van and three or four motorbikes parked in neat formation, the riders gathered nearby, drinking from polystyrene cups. As Charlie pulled up they all nodded and raised their cups in recognition.

Charlie and Amy dismounted and he pulled the bike on to its centre stand. Then he went over to chat. Amy stayed where she was, leaning against the bike with her arms crossed. Five minutes went by, then ten, the precious hour disappearing down the plughole. Charlie and the blokes were having a great laugh, throwing insults at the sniggering middle-aged man in the burger van. Amy stared at them sullenly then had an idea. Slowly, with feigned carelessness, she unbuttoned her denim jacket and threw it open to reveal the clingy white vest that she'd worn especially for the way it outlined her braless bosoms. Moving this way and that she stole a look at Charlie. He had his back to her, although the burger van bloke and two of the bikers were looking over with interest. Optimistically, she maintained the pose but Charlie didn't even glance at her.

By the time he came back, Amy was thoroughly depressed.

'Some mates from my old job,' he said. 'They worked for me on the City bypass. I had a hell of a job keeping them in line.'

'Right,' said Amy.

'Anyway,' said Charlie, stuffing his gloves in his helmet and hanging the lot on the handlebar. 'We don't have much time.'

And suddenly he was up against her, a chunky thigh pressed between her legs. 'Are you going to take your lid off or what?' he said.

Amy tore at the chinstrap, silently cursing its

fiddliness. Suddenly her head felt incredibly hot. Eventually she managed to rip the suffocating thing off. Gulping in fresh air, she handed it over, her ears singing.

With meticulous care he hung his wife's helmet over the other handlebar. Then with considerably less tenderness he pulled Amy's top down, picked up her naked breasts and began to squeeze and roll while rubbing his thigh muscle hard against her crotch.

Amy wished she could stop smiling but she couldn't help it. She noticed how he'd positioned himself so the other men couldn't see her tits, even though they were trying their best to cop an eyeful. How gallant of him, she mused, to guard her modesty. She couldn't stop looking at his face, his mouth slightly open, his breath coming more and more heavily as he watched the ever-changing shapes of her tits in his hands.

Looks-wise, she thought she and Charlie were a good match. They were both attractive without quite being beautiful, with enough imperfections to look human.

A downwards tug on his waistband brought his cock into the open air and she began to massage it, her hand a firm cylinder. Under the supple layer of skin it was solid. He began making low, thick noises through his nose. He definitely liked it hard and fast and before long she was pounding his pubis, the vibration travelling up her arm as he swayed his hips towards her with eyes closed, smiling to himself. He leaned forwards, grazed her neck with his teeth and murmured, 'Take your trousers off.'

'What, here?'

'It's OK, you're safe,' he said, with such reassuring warmth in his voice that Amy found herself trusting him completely. So she began surreptitiously to inch her trousers down, keeping her body very tight and narrow behind Charlie's frame. He was so well-built that it wasn't hard to hide behind him. In the background the blokes were falling about laughing but Amy didn't care. She wanted nothing between her and Charlie.

'Knickers,' he said. 'Get them off too.'

He helped her tug her trousers and underwear down her lower legs, leaving them hanging off one ankle. She sat on the warm bike seat and opened her legs.

'Little arrow,' he said with a nod.

Amy realised that the men could see her knickers. Glancing down she saw the gusset facing outward with its creamy stain for all to see. Quickly she reached down to flip it over but at that moment Charlie ploughed two fingers into her snatch, paralysing her. Cheeks burning, legs wide, all she could do was close her eyes and roll her head back, knowing this might be the only time Charlie would devote so much attention to her.

There was little noise apart from her breathing and

the smooching sound of her manipulated pussy. The sun was warm on her tits and thighs, encouraging her muscles to soften. Would he find engineering inspiration in the functions of her form? Perhaps she might be the next Stella Petterly, her head held high, her body a legend, her vagina the blueprint for a futuristic skyrail that achieved untold speeds by sliding on some new type of industrial lubricant.

Suddenly she became aware of a cold feeling between her legs. She opened her eyes.

Charlie was looking down at her pussy, his fringe hiding half his face. The bikers had moved in much closer. They were only a few metres away. Their eyes were all cast down, all trained on the same thing.

They were all staring at her pussy, and Charlie was holding her wide open for them.

Amy let out a horrified moan.

'It's OK, you're safe,' Charlie said again, then turned to the men, using both hands to splay her snatch.

Confused and humiliated, Amy didn't try to close her legs but stayed still, trying to get a handle on herself. There was a frightening seriousness on the faces of the bikers, who'd been joined by the burger van man and were edging closer. She felt nauseous but at the same time uncontrollably turned on. Betrayed not only by Charlie but by her own sluttish body, she realised she'd walked right into this one. Averting her eyes from her audience, she let out a shuddering sigh, trying not to think how desperate she was for an orgasm, how low she'd stoop to get one.

She looked down at her body, pink and stiffened, her pointy breasts spilling over the neckline of her vest, her pussy opened up by his fingers, the sight of it without its fur still a novelty to her so that, looking at it now, it seemed beyond naked. There was no hedge of hair to corral her juices and everything was wet, her mound, her labia, her legs, her arse, everything a glossy mess.

'They'd all like to enjoy you,' said Charlie.

'No,' she said weakly.

He stood upright and let go of her pussy.

'Charlie,' she whispered. 'It's you I want.'

'OK, but it's like I said –' he produced a foil packet '– it's a hell of a job keeping these boys in line. I can't make any promises.'

'Get a move on, Chaz,' said the burger man. His stained apron was flapping over his wanking fist.

'Lady says no, boys.'

They gathered round, flanking Charlie at both sides. Amy couldn't bear to look at their faces.

'Doesn't look like no to me,' said one.

A hand reached for her breast and Charlie slapped it away. 'You heard,' he said.

Amy was gratified that he was standing up for her. She had thought Charlie was going to throw her to them like butchered meat. But it seemed he could equally express his dominance like this.

'C'mon,' said another. 'Look at her. She's, like, literally dripping down your seat.'

'Sorry, boys,' said Charlie. His hands went down to her crotch again, busily opening her up, two fingers burrowing in. 'You can watch if you want.'

His cock was sticking out of his jeans, rude and presumptuous. She knew she'd be so grateful to have it inside her, no matter how badly Charlie treated her. As long as he fucked her as good and as hard as she needed.

Taking a deep breath she made herself look at her audience. And what she saw surprised her. They weren't quite the predatory faces that she'd half-seen through ashamed lashes. They were the faces of four ordinary men. One was short with a young-old face, a lined forehead and cropped, downy hair. One was a redhead with a wealth of freckles. One was a knuckle of a bloke, Eastern-Mediterranean looking, with a shaved head and a thick shelf of brow over a pair of twinkling black eyes. The burger man was the only one who really revolted Amy with his oily forehead and little turned-up nose. He was the only one masturbating, his tongue curled over his upper teeth, but judging by the congested looks on the others' faces, Amy guessed they all had stiff dicks under their leathers.

Each thrust of Charlie's fingers was accompanied by

that low nasal noise of his. He was giving a lot of stimulation to the front wall of her vagina, sparking some mouth-watering sensations, and Amy found herself thinking that it was the mark of a married man that he knew how to get the best out of a pussy.

She was quite shocked by her own callousness. But then, she reasoned, this was a callous situation. She'd made a play for a married man and it had backfired. He didn't want to have a proper affair. He didn't want to get to know her better. He didn't want to respect her. He wanted to use her to get one over on his mates. And it was OK. She would survive this minor disappointment in her life and, more than that, she would rise to the occasion.

'Like what you see?' she said to her audience and was amazed to see their eyes flick away, as if she'd embarrassed them. Just like that, she gained the upper hand. They were the ones with the pent-up arousal and the stiffies that had nowhere to go. She knew exactly where she was going.

She smiled and began to tease her clit with a circling finger. She'd never masturbated in front of anyone before. The men followed every tiny movement she made.

'Dirty bitch,' said the redhead. 'You just keep frigging yourself off.'

'I intend to,' she said, hips rolling.

The burger man was going for it under his apron.

Now the other bikers began to strip off their leathers so they could get to their pricks. Amy touched herself with the same slow intensity that she used when she was alone. She thought of all those recent occasions when, lying on her bed with her nightie pulled up, she would have given anything for Charlie to fill her hole.

Just as she was starting to quicken her circling, Charlie withdrew his fingers, wiped them in her hair, pulled her up close by her hips and pressed his cock at her entrance. She didn't try to meet his eyes. She extended her neck to get a good view of his dick pushing in. The circle of men shrank in closer. Amy couldn't help yelping when Charlie's dick reached its deepest point and somehow found the same erogenous area on her front wall that his fingers had brought to life. She hoped he wouldn't alter the angle and he didn't, slamming home again and again with the awesome accuracy of a man who'd been well instructed by his missus over the years.

It was clear that Charlie meant to give the boys a good show. Each time he withdrew he brought his gleaming cock almost the whole way out so that only the tip was still in her, before pushing forwards again with a violence that Amy thought would tip the bike over. She made sure she kept her legs wide, resisting the temptation to lock her ankles round him. She began to frig her clit more quickly, using two fingers, feeling it grow fatter by the second.

Now the redhead and the short guy were crouched on either side, their faces only inches away from Charlie's cock and her pussy. Their shoulders were shaking and Amy realised they were wanking. At Charlie's shoulder stood the burger man, looking down the length of his absurd little nose, while the knuckle stood a few metres away, filming the scene on his phone as he tossed himself off. There was heavy breathing all round her, with short grunts and muttered filth – 'Fucking slut' – 'Cock-hungry whore' – 'Sopping cunt can't get enough' – and it made her giddy, the lowness to which she'd sunk.

Tensing her legs, she realised she could easily have an orgasm. And frankly, she felt it was the least she deserved. Giving a special smile to the guy who was filming, she went for it with her fingers, creating maximum friction, wasting no time. She closed her eyes to concentrate then realised she preferred them open. Oddly, Charlie's were screwed tight shut. Whatever was emblazoned on the inside of his brain was enough to make his whole body rumble.

And just as she thought she was gone she was rudely disturbed by the ginger bloke jumping up and spraying hot semen across her belly. Seconds later the knuckle rushed over, one hand gripping his crimson cock, the other still filming. He took aim and shot his load at Amy, following the trajectory with his phone as it spattered her shoulder, her neck and finally her thigh. Amy looked down at herself, aghast, but she had hardly any time to assimilate what was happening before the short guy leaped to his feet and let fly a torrent of come. She turned her face away but not quickly enough because the stuff was in her ear, in her hair, plastered all over her cheek and chin. Charlie grinned cruelly, plunged his cock up her and froze in orgasm, apparently delighted by the sight of her covered in goo.

Amy watched the look of elation fade from his face as his climax ran its course. The shock made her forget her own orgasm for a moment but now she was determined to finish herself off. As the dicks around her softened, the men's expressions grew harder and colder. She saw them mentally regaining the upper hand. Resolutely, she stiffened her body, locked her legs and resumed her clitoral stroke. Looking down, she was astounded at the mess growing cold on her skin. The realisation of what she was doing made her ache in so many ways. Thoroughly degraded, the salty sting of sperm seeping into the corner of one eye, she brought herself off and, as she groaned with relief, the burger man stepped forwards – the one she'd forgotten all about – and, lifting his apron, squirted on her tits, first one, then the other, and methodically wiped his helmet in the ooze.

* * *

A week later, Amy handed in her notice. Andrew was concerned but Amy reassured him that she was fine, only she felt the need to take a risk and see what came her way.

Charlie didn't come to her leaving do. She drank immoderately, pole danced on a lamppost and swapped numbers with a black-haired boy called Steven who was training to be a teacher. Inspired, she decided she wanted to do the same thing and started applying for courses. Her friends and family were impressed with her new drive.

And when her dad came back from the pub one evening and told her poor Andrew had discovered that his wife was sleeping with one of his senior engineers, Amy knew who it had to be. That night she hardly slept, plagued by images. She saw Charlie smiling with a Buddha-like radiance as Stella tongued his erection before arching her back and spraying two white fountains all over him, hosing him down as he closed his eyes and opened his mouth in joyful welcome.

The following morning her university acceptance letter arrived. Amy was elated. Texting Steven the news, she decided that, next time she saw him, she'd fuck his brains out.

Slapper
Rachel Kramer Bussel

'I want you to slap your face for me. Go ahead, show me what you like.' His voice is deep and smooth, guiding me like a preacher, the kind of voice anyone would want to obey – at least, anyone submissive, anyone for whom such a voice is familiar and hypnotic and home. Or maybe just a girl like me, a girl for whom that voice, that command, that knowledge of what I want and what I'm scared of swirled together like a vanilla and chocolate ice-cream cone, one blending right into the other, makes me fiercely wet. It fires up my pussy like nothing else can. I'm certainly under his spell, because it sounds less like a command and more like something I was already planning to do and just hadn't become aware of yet.

I don't stop and think; I don't tremble or pause. I just

follow the voice belonging to the man on the screen of my laptop and close my eyes and slap my right cheek with my right hand. Because it's me doing it to myself, I think it won't hurt, won't sting, won't shock, but it does all of those things. I open my teary eyes and see the light handprint there and suddenly want to close them again – did I really just do that? – but he's staring right at me, as intensely as if we were physically in the same room. I know he's waiting to see how it felt, to see if I want more. Of course I want more; that's just how I'm built. And of course he knows that, and is not really waiting to see if I liked it; that was a foregone conclusion. He's waiting for me to acknowledge it, to say it, to let him know how well he gets me. I can pretend we barely know each other, as I did for the first few weeks, laughingly referring to it as a virtual fling, but now that it's been half a year, I can't deny that this is the kinkiest and somehow most solid relationship I've had, solid in that even if we don't stay together, I trust that he is as deeply invested as I am, that there's none of the usual confusion or unspoken uncertainties lurking between us. Once you've revealed yourself like this, you can't go back. He knows the important things, the things that turn every other aspect of my life inconsequential. He knows the girl behind the woman, the parts that need TLC just as much as they need complete surrender, and he knows those two go hand in hand, so to speak.

'How did that feel, Betty?'

'Good. But I wish you were here to do it.' It's true, even though we've never met in person, even though it did feel good – better than good, actually. The shock of it was different from being hit by someone else, but it was still there. I don't think I'm ever properly prepared for how sensitive the skin of my cheek is, how sensitive I truly am, and knowing exactly how twisted this makes me fuels my lust. Who likes being slapped? Isn't that what we're taught to avoid? Apparently, I do – very, very much, because just thinking about it makes the hair on my arms stand alert, makes me catch my breath and shiver with delight. The heat of the smack on my delicate skin, the way it captures me completely, body and mind, I love it all. Of course, being slapped by a man I'm beholden to, a man I crave and want and love, is something else entirely. It takes a special man, a caring man, a man who can overcome everything he's been taught about how to treat a lady to give his all to taking her cheek and making it a canvas for his handprints.

That's what so many 'dom' types I've seen online don't get – that it's not just about giving or taking orders, not just about the trappings, the look, the words. It's about seeing underneath all of those, peeling them back to expose your core, to tremble on the inside whether you're doing so on the outside or not. It's hard to do that when someone is working from a kinky script they learned from some mass-produced movie. It's the rare men I let expose me in this way. I can keep that armour in place even while sucking their cock on my knees with my hands tied behind my back, even while clamps are tightening around my nipples, even when the soles of my feet are being tickled until I want to laugh, scream and pee all at once, though I do none of them. The armour is like my superhero power, invisible to most. The ones who can unpeel it, that is their superhero power too; they can see it no matter what I do to hide. Their very presence makes it lighter, more transparent. They could tell me to smile and those words would be enough to make my insides melt, my body dissolve from mine to theirs in an instant, just with the sound of their voice – and the meaning behind it. The right order from the right man will make me give him everything. So a slap is never just a slap, and neither is a smile.

This man, Carter, this virtual stranger who knows me so well, understands all that. I'd bet my life on it. I don't need to have felt his breath heating the air between us, his hands digging into my skin, his weight holding me down, to know that. Whereas some might say you can't do kink from cross-country, I know the truth – that true submission is an act of the soul as much as the body, that it runs so deep that place becomes almost a quaint concept. Here, in this technology-aided intimacy, we have transcended place, transcended, or perhaps just bypassed, all the tropes that get in the way and boiled ourselves down to our purest essences. He sees everything about me through his 13 x 15 inch screen.

I'm not lying about any of that, I believe it with everything I've got in me, but I still want to smell him, taste him, feel him. If he can make my slap as visceral as if he were giving it to me by proxy, I can only imagine what he himself could do to me, what power he could bring to it. I've observed the way his sadism – which, when you think about it, has become kind of a sadistic word, with nothing in its two syllables to soften it just a touch to convey its pleasures – animates his face, turning it just slightly less handsome, more sinister. I've heard the way it turns his voice, not deeper and darker and dangerous – that's for those fake types I mentioned earlier – but lighter, softer, deceptively kinder. An unsuspecting girl might hear a carefree tone, but I know better. In his whispers I hear that his desire to hurt me runs as deep as my desire to be hurt, to be taken, to be owned. That is something you can't conjure, no matter how good an actor you are; plenty of vanilla boys have tried with me and failed.

I've seen his big, beautiful hands, the pale skin with the wisps of light-brown hair on the knuckles, the nails short but even, not too soft or too toughened. I've seen them typing, holding glasses and wrapped around his cock as he jerks off for me during our webcam chats. It scares me a little that they've felt more intimate than all the real-life relationships I've had. His hand is probably twice the size of mine, though I'm not a size queen about these things, because that is not really the point. You don't need a big hand to grab my hair, to edge a knife's blade along the curve of my breast, to pinch me in the places I don't want to be pinched but get wet when you do it anyway. When I try to explain to my friends the way Carter makes me feel, the way he sees inside me, the way he gets me almost better than I do myself, all they can think about is the distance. 'He's all the way across the country,' my best friend, Ali, will say. She'll acknowledge that he's cute, smart, even sexy, but those are not reasons to spend every night naked in front of my computer, glued to it, to him, drawn so magnetically I cannot imagine life without him even after such a short time. I could try to convey it all to her – she's open-minded enough – but that would start to peel those layers even my closest friends aren't privy to and may never be.

I know the truth – that we are as close as we want to be, as close as we believe ourselves to be. And right now I can feel his presence running from my stinging cheek all the way down, deep deep down, a sting that makes my pussy contract and my toes tingle. Mostly it makes me nervous that he knows exactly how much I love being slapped, so much that I'd do it to myself, something I've not only never done before but never even considered. It makes me nervous – and very, very turned on.

'Of course you do.' He says it so smoothly, so calmly, like he's always been able to see inside me. It's those four words that make me whimper, that make me blush. We haven't met in person yet, but we've shared so much, perhaps because of the distance, or because of the camera. It's created intimacy by proxy, a way of letting us spill our innermost secrets without fear. I've shared everything, even the things that make me cry, and the fantasies that make me blush. Sometimes I've looked away, whispered so softly he could barely hear, and had to type something in chat to him because it was just too much to say out loud. It's been six months, though, and we're reaching the point where we have to make a plan to see each other or we'll both be driven mad.

So his 'of course' makes sense, but still, there's a knowledge behind it that says so much more than those two little words, that innate knowledge of what I need to hear, of what makes perfect sense. I hear him mentally scanning through every depraved thought I've ever shared, every filthy fantasy, searching for one to play back to me. Most are dreams I've never gifted to any other lover because I wouldn't be able to look them in the eyes afterwards, would fear the judgment or, perhaps worse, desire staring back at me, and this is one instance where the distance has brought us closer. Carter will keep probing until I feel compelled to divulge all, yet I don't feel violated, but simply known, seen. He does not have a formula he wants me to follow, a right way or a wrong way. There is just my way and his way and the two are simply complementary paths to the same destination. He knows what I've told him, but he doesn't actually know, not really, not from experience, which makes his assurance all the more hot. That he can take control of me with his voice, with his knowledge, is what makes me fall over that fateful edge for him, right then, with those eight letters that tell me everything important about him. 'What would it be like if I were there to slap you?'

'You'd do it harder,' I say, feeling a blush heat up my cheeks. I dare to look directly into the camera, my spread legs shaking, but I keep staring, almost defiantly, waiting. Every time I look up at him – hell, every time I log on – I am admitting to both of us that I am choosing to spend my time like this, to devote myself to a man whom I have yet to kiss, to hold, to bed. I'm choosing him over the flesh-and-blood offerings in my vicinity because he has something they don't, and it's about far more than the ways I want him to torment me. He'd not only do it harder, he'd slap me, surely, in a way that left no room for doubt of his true feelings.

'I would, I can promise you that, Betty.' And I know it's true. The rest of the talk leaves me tingling and trembling and sure that we do have to make this a reality, test its possibilities.

* * *

Three weeks later, I'm in his bed, the queen-size one I've watched him in for all these months. It feels more than a bit surreal, and I'm more than a bit nervous. I knew I had to finally bite the bullet and get over my fears about taking what seemed so real into even more real territory, but now I can't help worrying that I've rushed things – ironic for a girl who's had more than her fair share of first-date sex. We are sitting up in his bed, me in the dress I wore specifically for the occasion, a pale-purple one that wraps around my neck and requires no bra, so the hardness of my nipples is very clear. My entire back is exposed, and the slight chill in the room is extra noticeable. I'm tempted to ask him what he wants me to do – isn't that always what girls ask? – but I simply wait and observe.

His room is very much a guy's room, full of comic-book paraphernalia and women in bikinis. I'm trying to surreptitiously observe. It smells like fresh air, though, perhaps because it gets an unusual amount of light. I guess I'd expected a musky cigarette smell, even though I know he's a fitness freak. Maybe he sprayed air freshener or something. Carter senses my fidgeting and grabs my hand. I expect him to put it on his cock, or shove it behind my back, but he just hold it, then tilts my face towards his, so we are staring at each other.

'Betty,' he says, his voice back to that deep, sexy rasp that makes me wet, so much so that I sense he could keep saying it over and over and I'd eventually come. It's different to not just hear it, but feel it in the air between us.

'Yes?' I whisper.

'Why are you here?'

He's not asking it like he wants to get rid of me, but to make me tell him, make me ask. 'I want you,' I say, and then I'm the one who moves so I can touch his cock. I've seen it so many times and I do want it.

'What do you want?' he asks, and the ache inside my centre deepens. I want him to stop asking and just take me, shove me on the floor or against the wall or simply spread me open and shove himself inside me – anywhere, everywhere. I want him to pinch me and bite me and slap me. I want him to use some of the many kinky toys I know he owns on me so that I'm bruised, marked, sore. I want something I couldn't get across my computer screen. But in the moment, I can't say all of that, or any of that. I bite my lip and am suddenly nervous our communication will go off course, that I've read too much into what he knows about me.

'You want me to slap that pretty face, don't you?' he

says after what feels like an interminable pause, as one hand shifts to a nipple, twisting it through the fabric of my dress, and the other curves around my bare cheek. The flat of his palm resting there makes me shiver, and he twists my nipple harder. My lips open as I inch closer to speaking. 'I think you should answer me, Betty, or I'll just have to find ways to amuse myself.' His hand slips under my dress to directly touch my nipple, and this time he is harsher, clamping down on it and compressing it until I think he can't possibly pinch it any harder, but the other hand remains in place, resting there softly, as if he's about to push a stray lock of hair behind my ear and simply got waylaid.

'Yes, Carter, I want you to slap my face – hard. As hard as you want to. I want you to make my cheeks red. I want you to make me cry.'

'Oh yeah?' he says softly, then raises his hand only to give me the gentlest tap, one that nevertheless startles me. I shiver and he smiles, a smile that sends chills through my body, followed by a rush of warmth as he releases my nipple only to claim it back immediately. 'I'll do that for you, Betty, because I know how badly you want it, but I have something else to do with my hands first. So you're going to have to show me again how you slap yourself. I want to watch you.' Then his hand is on my other nipple; he lifts both breasts over the edge of my dress, so it's propping them up, and tugs on them until they're straining away from my body. He twists them fiercely, not just the nipple but the surrounding skin, but for some reason, unlike my immediate, impulsive obedience over Skype, this time I'm hesitant. I came here for him to slap my face, not for me to do it just as well as I could at home, right?

But then I see the fierce look on his face, and realise that *this* is what I came here for: to have a battle of wills, and to lose – or at least, to win by losing. The longer I hold out, the more urgent his twists and tugs get, and I see the frustration on his face; I've never disobeyed him before. I can also tell he wants to slap me now, partly in kink and maybe just a little in frustration, to give in to what we both ultimately want, but is making himself wait to teach me a lesson. I didn't minor in topping from below for no reason.

'Do it, Betty,' he growls, and then I do – tilting my chin slightly up, I raise my right hand and bring it down on my cheek with a loud slap, the noise reverberating through the room. He drops his hands so they rest lightly against my legs and his eyes urge me to do it again. I do, the other hand, not my dominant one, this time. 'Do it like you want me to do it,' he commands, and I slap my right cheek as hard as I can. I'm shaking, not because he now so clearly knows how badly I want this, but because I'm so clearly under his spell. He could tell me to climb out his second-storey window naked and I probably would.

'More,' he says, 'until I tell you to stop.' And then I keep slapping my cheek, not robotically, but enough to get a little rhythm going. Each time it still stings, though not as much as the first. I close my eyes and my still-recovering nipples perk up – I wish he'd slap those too. But I focus on what I'm doing, what he's seeing, and before I know it, he's telling me to stop. I don't know how long it's been but I'm overwhelmed by his rough kiss. I am back to the innocent I once was, hoping I've served him well, hoping I'll get my reward. His kiss turns soft, gentle, tender, his tongue tickling mine.

And then he pulls his tongue out, grabs me by my hair, and slaps my left cheek. The tears immediately spring to my eyes and he slaps me again. Each blow was hard, stinging, and incredibly arousing. 'That's what you want, isn't it, my little pain slut? That's what you flew three thousand miles for, isn't it?' His voice is gruffer than I've ever heard it, and his hand has shifted from my hair to my arm, where it's clasped tightly in his grip.

'Yes, Carter, yes, I want you to slap my face, my tits, my pussy.' I hadn't meant to say the last – I'd never told him that – but it didn't escape his notice.

'I bet I could bring my friends over and you'd love for them to slap you too,' he says as he gives both of my cheeks the beating I've been craving. When he holds one cheek against his palm and slaps me with the other, the sting of it penetrates even more deeply. I whimper out something that sounds like 'yes' even though we've discussed the truth: that all I want is Carter, that I'll do the most outrageous things with him, for him, but ever since we started talking, other people have been off my radar. I only have room for him, and I think he suspects this, but wants to tease me anyway. He slaps me again and I try to drop my head down just a little, but his hand is there, firm and steady, keeping me in place. 'You want me to slap your pussy now, don't you? You want me to spank you right here?' he asks, pinching my clit before giving me a light slap there. 'I think I'll have to tie you up for that; can't have you squirming around too much and not getting the full treatment. Do you want me to tie you to my bed, Betty? I showed you the cuffs I bought, and where I'd secure you.' It was true; he'd given me a guided tour of his four-poster bed, as well as all sorts of torturous implements he owned, though my favourite one was attached to his arm.

This is different, though. I've never been tied up like that, fully exposed, from my armpits to my pussy to the soles of my feet. There'll be no hiding, no flinching, no covering myself. 'Yes, I do, I want you to tie me up and spank me all over. Spank my pussy, and my tits,' I say, and even though I'm more like 95 per cent rather than 100 per cent sure as I utter the words, hearing them out loud and picturing myself strung up makes my pussy clench so tightly I think I'll scream.

Instead I calmly lie down on my back and let him take me, one wrist at a time, one ankle at a time. Efficiently, Carter secures me in padded leather cuffs and attaches them to hooks on each bedpost. 'I could gag you, but I want to hear you scream,' he says. I almost laugh, because in another context that could sound like something out of a horror movie, but the way he says it makes me wet. Having my pussy clench when I was sitting was one thing, but having it clench and my inner thigh muscles tighten while I'm spread wide like this is completely different. It feels like Carter can see every thought racing through my mind, like he knows me truly inside and out. He climbs on to the bed and tickles his way up my right leg with his fingertips. I shiver, until he places his palm over my pussy – then I bite my lip, not in fear, simply in anticipation. I've had my pussy slapped before, but never while I was tied up.

Then that first glorious blow lands, an explosion of heat against my most tender body part. I shiver all over and my first instinct is to try to stop him, to put my hand there, which is what I'd do if my hands weren't tied up. He runs a finger along my slit and then spanks me there again. And again. Each time I can feel myself getting wetter, can feel that wetness leaking out of me, making itself known. There's no escaping this even if I wanted to. Carter puts a hand over my mouth and then swats at my breasts, coming at them from the side, then hitting my nipples head on. I do what instinct tells me to do, and push against him. He pushes back harder, and turns my face on to its side. I shift my body as much as I can, which isn't much, and am soon dying to have something in my pussy – his fingers, his cock, I don't care what. I want it so, so badly, but I can't ask for it, because if I do he'll surely deny me.

My tears pop up unexpectedly, but they are welcome, a way to relieve some of the intensity coursing through my body, overtaking every inch of me. Carter pinches each nipple once, hard, then raises my head to face him. My cheeks are wet, but that doesn't stop him slapping the right one, then holding his hand close and tapping the same spot, before giving it another whack. He does it again and for a second I want to ask him to stop, but, like magic, the moment I'm about to open my mouth is the moment my body changes its mind and wants another slap. He gives it to me, then one on the other side. He slaps me for what feels like minutes but is probably less than one. By the end my sex is so swollen and aroused it's almost painful.

Carter doesn't say anything, just quietly uncuffs me, then kisses me deeply as he eases his body on top of me. He's already wearing a condom, and he places his cock where he wants it, then presses inside. He doesn't warn me, but he doesn't need to. His cock is my reward for getting through all those smacks – although they were a reward in and of themselves. Carter pauses, with his cock buried deep inside me, to look at me. I'm sure my hair is every which way and my face covered with more emotions than I can even process at the moment. But he simply leans down and kisses the cheek he slapped so many times just a few minutes ago. He keeps his lips there, resting lightly against my warm skin, as he takes me somewhere new and beautiful – somewhere I never could've gotten to across my computer screen. I wrap my legs around him, grateful they are free, and that we've found each other. There will be time for more slaps later, I'm sure; for the moment, his breath on my cheek and our bodies wrapped around and around each other are more than enough.

Love Bites
Chrissie Bentley

When a night of vague nostalgia convinced me to add my name and address to one of those 'old friends reunited' websites, I never expected anything to come of it. I'd keyed in my old high school, recognised maybe six names in the list and joined the club out of curiosity more than anything else. Then I changed my mind and tried to get out, but the complexities of cyber-registries have never been one of my strongest points. I braced myself for another storm of poorly spelled emails offering sex aids and pharmaceuticals, and forgot all about it. Until about a month ago.

I was trashing spam when a name in an email address rang a vague bell just as I hit 'delete'. I punched 'restore' and double-checked: Lawrence.Bacon@. Hey, I knew a Lawrence Bacon, but it was one helluva long time ago.

Lawrence Bacon was the first guy I ever slept with. I was seventeen, he was twenty; we met at the office where I was working evenings, and were together for a year, until he left me for some blonde whom he met at a club. I'd like to say I was broken-hearted – in fact, I may have been for a week or two (the mind blocks out the memory of those sobbing phone calls late into the night), but I soon got over it, got over him, got on with the rest of my life. And now, all these years – ahem, decades – later, I clicked 'open' and I knew it was him straightaway. 'I was doing a search for friends I'd lost touch with; I was so thrilled to find you on the site,' and so on in a similar tone of delight, as if it was just a few weeks, not years, since the last time he'd so much as looked at me.

I hit reply, and responded in kind: 'Great to hear from you. ...' blah blah blah, 'what are you doing ...' gush gush gush. And I tried to imagine what he'd look like now. People say, look at the father if you want to know how the son will turn out, and Lawrence's pop really wasn't that bad for his age. I shuddered at a sudden thought: the last time I saw Mr Bacon he was probably younger than I am now. Which means Lawrence would be even older – mid-forties. Was he married, were there kids? I wondered how long it would take for him to write back; suddenly I found myself feeling very curious indeed.

Over the next few days we exchanged all manner of

details. He was divorced; he had children, a daughter who was away at university in England, and a son who'd just returned. Holy shit, even his kids were older than he was when we'd been together. Where the hell does the time go these days? He was still living in the same town as well. I'd drifted a clutch of counties over since then, but we arranged to meet, and all day my mind kept meandering back to the time we spent together and forced me to admit that, once past the sex, I really couldn't remember anything.

I was still a virgin when we had first started dating and, though things certainly improved with practice, I hoped Lawrence had more understanding recollections of our first time than I did. You've heard people describe embarrassing moments of their lives as 'not my finest hour'; between the panic, the pain and the sheer discomfort of a piece of carpet in the back of a van, this was not my finest ten seconds.

But there were good times as well, such as the first time he ever went down on me. I was absolutely astonished. Of course I knew all about it; like most healthy seventeen-year-old girls, I'd already read my fair share of articles, and even seen a few dirty movies, hijacked from my girlfriends' brothers when they were off doing boy things. But I was certain that those were the only places where guys actually did things like that and, as Lawrence's tongue had traced its way down my belly and thighs, as I realised with amazement that he was closer towards my pussy, I don't know what shocked me the most: that it was actually happening to me, or that it was happening in such a normal room, in a normal house, in an excruciatingly normal town.

On the street outside, I heard a car drive past. Could the people inside have even dreamed what was occurring just twenty feet and a few walls away from them? Could they have ever *dreamed* that I was lying there with my legs spread, and a tongue teasing around my cunt lips? And would they have believed it if they could?

He brushed my clitoris, and I almost screamed as I felt that nerve-jangling flicking for the first time, and every tiny movement of his lips and tongue sent a new spasm of ecstasy rushing through me. Desperate not to let the moment pass, I asked, no, begged, Lawrence to bite me there. Harder, please harder. Pleeeeeease.

He bit.

It hurt like hell, and I knew it would continue hurting for days to come, but that was the point. For as long as I could feel the stinging, I'd be able to remember that *my* quim had been in *his* mouth, for a few voluptuous moments before he kissed his way back up my belly, then slid his cock inside me.

The memory flashed away, to be replaced by another one. Months passed, and we were fucking regularly, but his teeth remained a hard, sharp focal point of our lovemaking, long after I lost the need to feel them. In fact, it was getting to the point where I was actually dreading him licking me, because there was very little licking even taking place. Boys get blow jobs; I was getting bite jobs, and my pussy was sore and bruised from his attentions.

I suppose I could have asked him to change his tactics, but, like I said, I was young, and worried that if I asked him to stop, he might get angry and never touch me again. One night, however, was different; one night, he treated me to a true eating-out: warm, wet and rhythmic, with all the smooth, loving gentleness and sense-shattering expertise that that entails. And, when I came – for the first time in his face – he clenched my ass and held me tight to his face, so that my frenzied gyrations smeared juice all over him. And, when it was over, and I lay back in absolute bliss, he raised himself and looked me in the eyes. Then he whispered, 'You're delicious.' All I could reply, as I lay in total shock, was 'So are you.'

The following week, he dumped me.

A quarter of a century later, that last night together remained my most powerful memory of Lawrence, a warm tongue that probed deep and relished every flavour I could give him, then drew me softly to a stupendous orgasm. It came to mind when I masturbated sometimes, one of those special moments that we all hold so dear, long after we've lost touch with every other moment we spent with a person. The one-night stand who wanted to lick his own come from my pussy; the way another loved me to milk him with my tits; the night I spent sucking a truck driver's dick: magical moments that you share with one lover, which can never truly happen again, no matter how many more times you do them. As I drove slowly into the tree-lined driveway of Lawrence's townhouse, I wondered what he'd think if he knew of his exalted place in my sexual hall of fame. He'd probably be thrilled.

My finger was still on the bell when the door swung open and, for a moment, I just stared. You know how it's considered polite to tell someone that they haven't changed a bit, no matter what the toll of the passing years? In Lawrence's case, it was true. His hairstyle was different, of course, but the laughing eyes, the dancing smile, the nose that sloped to a gentle button, the dimple. 'Lawrence?' I said.

'You wish!' came a voice from behind him. The boy who answered the door ducked and smiled. Lawrence appeared in the doorway. 'I thought that would freak you,' he said with a laugh, and I saw him quickly look me up and down. 'You, on the other hand ...'

I brushed aside the rest of his platitude and stepped into the house. A few pieces of furniture looked familiar; a couple of photos of elderly relatives. And Lawrence, of course, looked as gorgeous as ever, even if the years had greyed his hair some, and etched a few wrinkles. I was surprised to find myself feeling pleased that the vision who opened the door wasn't him. Youth is a beautiful thing, but it can be damned intimidating, too, and the sight of that boy's unlined face, fresh smile and smooth skin made me feel even older than I am.

We sat in the front room, Lawrence balanced on the arm of the sofa, while I sat beside him and his son, Brian, sprawled on the floor, looking up at the pair of us with a huge smile. 'You know, I can see the pair of you together. I always know when two people have that attachment, and you two really do.'

Lawrence laughed embarrassedly. 'It was a long time ago, a very long time ago. I'm sure Chrissie barely even remembers.'

'Hey, you were my first great love,' I protested. 'I remember everything.'

'Everything?' asked Lawrence, his laugh still on his lips.

'Everything?' echoed Brian with a sense of wonder adding emphasis to his words, and I saw Lawrence flash him the kind of look that can only pass between two men who've shared some kind of secret.

'Actually, I doubt that very much,' Lawrence concluded. 'I'm the one who remembers everything. You just hang on to the weird stuff.'

Well, he got that bit right, I thought, then asked with

a chuckle, 'So what have you been telling people? Which one of our sordid little secrets is now pinned with a magnet to your fridge door?'

Lawrence spoke first. 'Remember that night we were walking home from some club and you couldn't wait for a pee, so you ducked into the graveyard?'

Then it was Brian's turn. 'Or the time – do you mind, Dad? – when you got your ear pierced and it swelled up to the size of a strawberry?'

'A raspberry,' corrected his father. 'It looked just like a raspberry.'

I racked up my mind for ammunition. 'OK, Brian, did he tell you about the night we went out for shellfish, only for him to remember, too late, that he was allergic to it? He was throwing up all night.'

'Like you at that party, after you got into that absurd drinking competition with those punk rockers,' Lawrence countered. 'But let's eat. Otherwise Brian will start thinking our entire relationship revolved around vomit, and I'm sure there was more to it than that.' He smiled and squeezed my arm. 'Come on, I've made your favourite.'

It was, as well. Although how he remembered that after 25 years, I dared not even ask. I couldn't even recall what brand of cigarette he used to smoke.

We small-talked through the meal; then settled back on the settee, only this time – and I'd swear it was at Brian's silent prompting – Lawrence sat firmly down next

112

to me, so close that I could smell his aftershave and, beneath that, the personal scent that, again, I'd forgotten, but which gave me instant crazy flashbacks to long ago, innocent days.

'So tell me again how you met,' Brian asked, and, laughingly, Lawrence and I turned back the years, to reminisce about an office that we'd not seen in 25 years, the awful people with whom we'd been working, and how we were thrown together as much from a need to put up a united front – the two youngest people in the office – as out of any kind of spoken attraction. But it was there all the same and, one evening as we were preparing to leave, he asked me out for a drink. 'And we were together for the next thirteen months,' said Lawrence proudly, 'right up until I met your mother.'

I had my drink to my lips as he said that; I truly hoped no one saw me splutter and, as I stifled a cough, spit my mouthful of wine back into the glass. 'You married that girl?' I could not help but ask. Lawrence nodded. 'I'm afraid so. And fifteen years later, I finally realised why you disliked her so much.'

Brian hissed a half-dismayed 'Dad,' but Lawrence hushed him. 'It's true. Chrissie couldn't stand your mother, called her a ... well, let's just say she didn't have a very high opinion of her. And, I'm afraid to say, she may have been right. But, as they say, I got two lovely children out of her, so it wasn't a complete waste of time.'

I was dying to ask what happened – the girl had been a tramp, quite frankly, one of those bottle-blonde trollops with huge tits, the legs of a giraffe and a pussy that could have doubled as the Harlem Tunnel, she'd had so many guys drive through her. I'm astonished she ever married, settled down, had kids. Although the fact that she wasn't here any longer suggested that maybe she hadn't. But now was not the time to pry.

Lawrence reached for the bottle and refilled my glass. 'Brian probably thinks I'm talking too much. I'll get a right telling-off in the morning. And, in fairness to Tina, she wasn't all bad. But I do know, and I've told Brian this, there were things that you and I did during our time together, Chrissie, that I could never have repeated with Tina, no matter how hard I tried.'

'Like what?' I asked, and I saw Brian's eyes flash a vivid warning to his now plainly intoxicated father. Lawrence caught the look as well. 'Let's just say, there were things. Now, if you'll excuse me, I must run to the bathroom.'

He rose unsteadily to her feet, and left Brian and me in silence. Finally the boy spoke. 'I'm sorry about that. He's been so nervous about you coming over tonight, I think he may have drunk a little more than he ought to.'

'Nervous?' I asked.

'Well, you've not seen each other for so long; who knew if you'd even like each other any more? Plus, I think he always remained just a little in love with you.'

I was surprised to hear those words, but not especially shocked at what they imparted. Just as Lawrence was my first great love, I was his, and that's one relationship you never really get over. 'That little exchange between the two of you, just then. The looks. Is that what that was all about?'

Brian flushed. 'I told you, he's been nervous; getting back in touch with you stirred up a lot of memories for him, from before he met my mom – and maybe some regrets as well.'

'Regrets?'

'Oh, I don't mean he wished he'd married you instead. But I think he'd have liked to have remained unmarried a little longer and, if you'd stayed on the scene, who knows?'

'He ditched me,' I protested. 'I didn't want to end it at all – especially not at that time!' I smiled to myself. That 'you're delicious' remark really had made a serious impression on me!

'I know,' Brian answered. 'Like I said, he sometimes wonders whether he maybe made some bad decisions.' He paused. 'Hold on, he's coming back. So –' deftly changing the subject '– I completed my Masters, and now I'm just waiting for a vacancy to come up at the museum, and I should be back in Egypt by Christmas.'

'My son the archaeologist,' trilled Lawrence as he walked back into the room. 'One mummy wasn't good enough for him, so he has to go and dig up some more.'

Ouch – he *was* drunk. He picked up the bottle and tilted it towards me. 'More?'

'I'd better not, I have to drive home tonight.'

'It's a bit late to be thinking about that,' Brian admonished me light-heartedly. 'We've already got through four bottles, and there's still two more to come. Dad, shall I run and make up the spare room?'

Lawrence looked at me questioningly. 'Should he?'

I hesitated for a moment; I could call a cab, then get another one back in the morning, to pick up the car, but it would be a lot easier if ... 'Well, if it's not too much trouble.'

'Not as much trouble as trying to explain to Highway Patrol why you're smashed out of your skull.' And then, to Brian, 'Yes, do that. And bring back another bottle when you're done.' Brian left, and Lawrence took my hand. 'I'm sorry, I didn't say too much, did I?'

'Not at all. In fact, I was rather hoping you'd say more.'

I swear he blushed a little. 'It's like I said, you do some things in one life, and no matter how hard you try in another, you just can't.'

'Like?' Half of me was certain that it knew precisely where this conversation was headed; the other half was braced for disappointment, in case he dredged up another memory altogether. Instead, he took the third option. 'No, you'll think it's silly. It was nothing.'

'You obviously don't think so.'

'No. Well, I wouldn't.'

'I'll ask Brian then.'

Lawrence punched me playfully. 'There are some things that even a son doesn't know. Thank God.' He leaned forwards and kissed me on the lips, paused and then kissed me harder. My mouth opened a little, and I felt his tongue flick in and around, then break away. 'I'll tell you one thing, though, you still taste delicious.'

My heart leaped and, even before it had landed, I felt my puss flooding inside my panties. And I mean flooding. 'So do you,' I breathed. 'And if you think that was nothing, or silly, believe me, I remember it like it was yesterday.'

His eyebrows arched curiously. 'Now you've got me wondering. What do you remember?'

Oh shit. As fast as my heart had started trip-hammering, it stopped, and I was still trying to formulate an answer that wasn't a stammered blur when Brian walked back in. 'I hope I'm not interrupting,' he teased.

'No, but you might be able to help me wring an answer out of Chrissie here. Now, what is this thing that you remember like yesterday?' Lawrence said.

Standing behind me, Brian started up a whispered chant, 'Tell, tell, tell.'

'Well, if you're going to gang up on me, I'll just have to go to bed.' I pouted, but Lawrence's grip on my hand was a strong one.

'Oh, if you think that'll get you out of it, you've got another think coming,' he said. And then: 'I may be old, but I still have my own teeth.'

Brian whooped delightedly. 'Father!' he roared with mock shock. 'I thought you were joking about that!'

What? I couldn't believe my ears. 'Lawrence? Now I really want to know what you've been telling him.'

'Why? I thought it was rather fun.' He lunged towards my face, snapping his teeth at me. 'Nothing wrong with a bit of biting. So long as you know where to bite.'

Behind him, Brian was convulsed with giggles. 'Father, I'm ashamed of you. And Chrissie ... I'd never have guessed!'

'I was young and in love,' I protested.

'Apparently so.' Brian smiled. 'But I think I should leave you two alone now; I'm sure I'd only be in the way.' He hung in the doorway for a moment. 'I'm going to run next door to see Kerry. Don't wait up.'

'Don't worry, we won't,' called Lawrence. Then, as the door slammed closed, he kissed me again. 'So now you know what I was talking about. Oh, and don't worry about Brian, he thinks I was talking about all the hickeys I used to give you. I told him how you went out and bought all those turtlenecks to cover them up at work, and then got into trouble for not wearing a blouse. But I couldn't help myself.' Again that phrase. 'You were so delicious. Now you have to tell me what you meant.'

I stroked his hair. 'To be honest, I think it was the exact same thing.' And that, apparently, was all the encouragement he needed. He slipped off the couch and on to his knees, then parted my legs with his hands and reached for my thighs. He tugged at my panties beneath my dress and I raised myself slightly and felt them fall free, hitched up my legs as he pulled them down to my ankles, then hoisted his hands beneath my ass to draw me to his face.

I was dripping wet; I caught a whiff of my own odour as I shifted, and then his face plunged into my folds, his tongue delving deep, his cheeks delightfully rough on my most tender flesh.

'I am so glad,' he purred, then stopped and looked at me. 'It's been so long. You know,' he said thoughtfully, 'not that there's been a lot of them, but you're the only girl who's ever let me do this.'

For a moment, I wondered who on earth he'd been sleeping with all these years. What sort of girl doesn't let a guy go down on her? And then – Ouch! Then I realised precisely what he meant. I was the only girl who let him bite her clit, hard, harder and harder still, until the pain was almost unbearable and it felt as though his teeth were going to slice right through it.

I gritted my teeth, determined not to spoil a moment that he'd evidently been waiting for, maybe even dreaming about, since the day he first walked out on me, and

119

prayed that his jaw would tire before he did me some serious damage.

But I let out a groan, and that was clearly a mistake, as he mistook my agony for enjoyment and his teeth dug in even deeper. And then, as suddenly as it began, the pain went away, and he was sucking, his lips drawing my flesh deep into his mouth, his tongue slipping up and down my labia lips and darting around my clit. Occasionally, he paused and his teeth dug in once again, but now I could deal with it, knowing that the seconds of excruciating pain would soon be rewarded with minutes of exquisite pleasure.

He was sucking as I started to come; he was biting as I did so, and I wondered how he was able to do that, crushing my clit with his teeth as his mouth filled with my juices. But he did it and, when he finally released me, the tingling of my orgasm combined with the savage pain of all that had precipitated it to crash against my body in a wave of sensations I had never felt before.

He kissed me, and I tasted myself smeared across his lips and tongue. 'See, I told you I remembered everything.' He smiled. 'Even how hard you come when I bite you like that.'

I kissed him back, and smiled to myself: maybe he was right when he said that I only remembered the weird stuff. But at least I remembered it correctly.

I wasn't about to correct him, however, and I still

haven't. I'd not come that hard in so long I don't recall, but I've been back with Lawrence for three weeks now, and now it happens almost every time we meet. Even better, he told me something else last weekend, about how biting doesn't need to be a one-sided thing. And the first time I sank my teeth into his hard, throbbing cock, after licking and swirling my tongue round his glans, I almost choked on the hot, thick and flavoursome come he squirted down my throat.

But that, I'm afraid, is another story.

Soaked and Dripping
Valerie Grey

I stood in the room with the other girls and thought: I'm crazy.

I had let my girlfriends in the dorm talk me into this.

The temptation was too great so I had to do it.

JoAnne, Heather and Amanda thought it would be a great idea for us to participate in the wet T-shirt contest at this bar off campus; but when I signed up for it they backed out and left me to do it alone.

I knew, then, they had set me up; this was planned. They knew about my exhibitionist tendencies and they wanted to exploit them.

I looked at the T-shirt that I had been given; looked at the other girls who obviously had done this before or had seen one before. They were busy cutting their shirts down and trimming them to be more revealing. The shirts had the bar logo on them, sold to customers for $10.

Had no idea what to do. Wasn't even feeling very good about taking off my top and bra in front of them.

One of them noticed the flabbergasted expression on my face and walked over to me. 'First time in one of these?' she asked.

'Yeah … what do I do?'

'Give me your shirt and I'll fix it up for you.'

I handed her my T-shirt and watched her cut off the sleeves with scissors. She cut the trim at the neck and held it up to me. She nodded to herself. She cut off a good chunk on the bottom and handed it back to me.

'Just get this on, and when you get on the stage, go with the flow. The guys out there will be happy with just about anything. Drunk lugs all of them.'

'Walking cocks,' another girl said, and several laughed.

I smiled nervously and turned my back to the room. Took off my top and bra and slipped the T-shirt on. Looked down and saw that it didn't cover much of me. There was a wide strip of my skin between the bottom and my shorts.

Turned back to the room and looked at the other girls. Was glad that I was small on top. Some of the girls were pretty big in the chest, and when they were wet their boobs were going to be pretty obvious.

Bent down and took off my shoes, wanting to keep

them dry. Sat on a chair and waited for my name to be called, hoping to be the last or that the MC would not have my name so I wouldn't have to go out there.

Who was I kidding? Deep down, I wanted to get on that stage and show off what I had to a horde of complete strangers.

One by one, names were called and we could hear music and cheers through the walls of the room. As each one came back I looked at them. They were soaked and you could see their nipples.

Was trying to remember everyone from my school that had come to this bar, but I couldn't remember anyone but my three so-called friends who had backed out on me. If I saw any guys that I knew, or even girls other than my friends, I was going to be pretty damned embarrassed. Hell, who was I kidding? I was going to be embarrassed anyway.

Wished that I was back at the dorm or maybe that I had drunk more. Wasn't alcohol supposed to suppress your inhibitions?

Heard my first name called and I almost jumped. I looked at the door and a big muscular man was motioning to me. He took my arm and led me to some stairs leading to a stage.

Could hear cheering and screaming and I nervously walked up the stairs. Another big muscular man took my arm and led me to the corner of the stage where a thin guy with long hair was waiting with a water hose. They faced me into the corner and sprayed cold water all over the back of the shirt and my shorts.

It was freezing!

I was turned around and he sprayed my chest and the front of my shorts. Soaking wet, my hand was taken again and I found myself at the centre of the stage. Music was blaring behind me and I could see a sea of faces out there, screaming and cheering. Mostly men of various ages. Some women.

I let my body's natural responses kick in gear; the deep bass of the music vibrated through my bones: started dancing and let my legs and body take over. Looked down and saw that my nipples were quite erect from the cold water. They were poking against the fabric and I blushed, realising how visible they were.

JoAnne, Heather and Amanda were yelling in front of me; they were at the centre of the stage, down on the floor, and I could barely see them with the lights in my eyes. There were shouts like 'Show your tits!' and 'Take it off!' from the crowd. Heather yelled, 'Get naked, slut!'

Tried to focus on the faces in front of me and to shake my wares as best I could. It was starting to become a rush, with all the guys cheering and yelling; I could feel myself getting wet at the thought of what was going on their minds. Were they fantasising about taking me on the pool table, on the floor, in the back alley? I was like a dangling carrot of desire and to have so many guys cheering because I was on stage felt good, did wonders for my ego.

I turned and let them see my butt in my soaked shorts and moved my ass cheeks for them, getting even more cheers; they kept yelling 'Show your tits!' but I was *not* going to do that, not for anyone.

I did put my hands over my boobs and simulated squeezing them and that got real good applause from the guys. I was *really* starting to get into this. I had never got this much attention before in my life. Why had I never done this before? This was not demeaning, I realised, but empowering – I could control the crowd with my body, I had the power to give or deny what they wanted.

This control was more intoxicating than alcohol. I didn't need to be drunk to strut my stuff on stage.

I kept dancing and swaying my hips and tried to shake my tiny boobs for them – I mean, I didn't have the natural jiggle some women have.

Then the music was gone and the MC stood next to me, his arm around my shoulders. He asked my name, my school and some other things I forget, I was so aped on adrenaline. I realised I was really wet between the legs but even if showed it didn't matter because my shorts were drenched in water anyway.

The MC held his microphone so everyone could hear my answers. Then he asked me if I was going to show my tits to the crowd. I giggled and shook my head. 'No way!' I said.

How little did I know my friends and their plans for me. He asked me again, trying to get me to flash, but I kept saying no, no, no, Joe. For every different way he asked, I shook my head and smiled sweetly. The crowd playfully booed. Then he told me to remember that it was a three-round contest with $500 going to the winner; he announced my name again to the crowd and I walked off the stage.

I was not going to show anything for any amount of money, I thought. What I was doing was enough to keep my friends off my ass. At least *I* got on stage, they had backed out.

I went to the backstage room and looked around. There were seven girls remaining now, soaked and dripping. Some were looking as shy as me, others a little more blatant. Felt I was holding my own. Wrung some of the water out of the shirt and the girl who had helped me came over.

'How do you feel?'

'I don't know. It was sort of a rush to be up there,' I told her. 'Was figuring I was going to be mostly embarrassed but I'm excited too.'

'All those hot guys, I *know*.'

I didn't know if they were hot …

'I'm definitely getting laid good tonight,' she said

'What happens now?' I asked.

'There are two more rounds, so we'll have to go up two more times, then the crowd will be asked to vote. Then one of us will be the winner, second, and third place. I'm Missy, by the way.'

We shook wet hands.

'Who do you think will win?'

She said, 'Whoever is willing to do the most on stage.'

'I don't understand.'

'Some of these girls will show their tits and some may even take off their shirts. Whichever one is the boldest will win.'

I must have looked like a fish out of its bowl, and like a cartoon, my mouth was open so wide, agape, eyes bulging,

Me: 'You can't be serious!'

She: 'Oh, yes, at least one, probably two or three or will take off their shirts. For five hundred dollars, won't you?'

Me: 'Absolutely not!'

I was naive.

Didn't figure on how mean my friends could be.

* * *

The girls' names were called and they went on stage to the thundering roars and cheers; seemed like there were more people out there than before.

I sat on my chair and watched as they came back. The first two came through the door and I could see that their shirts were torn down the front. Then the third one came back topless. I couldn't *believe* that a girl would do that. The fourth came back with her shirt in one piece and then the fifth was topless.

I was getting nervous again. Missy had gone on stage for her turn and I knew that I would be next. Even with my nerves, I resolved to go through with this. My friends would tease me unmercifully if backed out now.

Missy came back with her shirt torn down part-way and it was now my turn. I swallowed my fear and marched up to the stage. Once again I was sprayed back and front and in no time I was centre stage again, hearing 'Show your tits, show your tits,' like a chant. I smiled as sweetly as I could as I started dancing.

Out of the corner of my eye, I saw JoAnne, Heather and Amanda being boosted up on the stage by some guys. As soon as they were with me, they converged on me and started dancing with me. I felt a little better with them there at first, until Amanda got a grip on my arms. I was starting to turn my head to tell her to let go when someone grabbed the top of my T-shirt and tore it down the middle. I shrieked and felt the cool air hit my nipples like a slap in the face. The shirt was pulled down off my shoulders and left hanging behind my back.

My boobs were completely uncovered.

JoAnne grinned at me then she spoke. 'Keep dancing. Just keep dancing.'

Amanda still held my arms and I tried to get away and cover up but she was stronger than I was. Heather took one of my arms and the two of them moved to my sides. JoAnne was dancing in front of me, with me, and she smiled at me nastily. She reached for the button on my shorts. They were holding me so I couldn't get away and couldn't stop them. Heather's hand went up my arm and she pulled the shirt off that arm. Quickly Amanda did the same and she tossed the shirt into the crowd. I was hearing a roar of approval from the guys in front of me. I tried to get away from JoAnne and by now she had my shorts unbuttoned. With all the water that had been sprayed on them, they were sagging and my panties were showing. JoAnne's hand grabbed my zipper and I felt it slide down.

My shorts were hanging on my hips ...

Then Amanda and Heather grabbed them on each side and pushed down. The shorts slid down my legs until they were pooled around my ankles and my panties were the only things I had on. The roar got louder and louder. Amanda and Heather bent down and they lifted one foot, then the other and got my shorts off me completely. Now I was hearing the crowd yelling, 'Show your bush, show your bush.' Amanda lifted my shorts above her head and twirled them around, and then she tossed them into the crowd. I was so red-faced. JoAnne pushed me up to the front of the stage and then the three of them quickly slipped off the stage into the crowd once more. I stood with my hands over my boobs and blushed so much. My panties were full of water too and were sagging and I didn't know if I should grab them with one hand and try to cover my boobs with the other. But even with my embarrassment, I was getting a rush of pure power. I knew that every one of the guys out there wanted me and me alone now. They wanted me to show my tits and even more. I certainly wasn't going to do that, but the excitement I felt was exhilarating. The MC was asking me to show my tits. I turned and let them see my butt with my soaked panties sagging down. I wasn't sure, but I thought the top of my butt crack was showing. I rolled my hips and let my butt shake for them. I was enjoying this too much. Finally, I turned back to the crowd and slowly let my hands slip down. I was showing my tits! Even if they were little ones, the guys seemed to like them and the roars of approval was music to my ears. I was excited, very excited. I danced a little bit, showing them what they wanted to see and then dashed off the stage to loud roar of approval. When I entered the room, the girls stared at me in my panties and some glared at me. My friend came over to me.

'Not going to show off? You sure surprised me.'

I said, 'Can't believe I'm doing this!'

'Where are your shorts?'

'Oh shit! One of my friends threw them into the crowd!'

'Hope that you don't want them back, because you will never see them again.'

I knew she was right. My shorts were gone for ever. I looked around for my top and bra and couldn't find them.

'I left them there,' I said

'A blonde came in here and took them,' Missy said.

Heather!

'This is all I have to wear,' I said.

We both looked at my soaked underpants. The first girl was called and she left and I tried to wring the water out of my panties. The other girls stared at me, some with hostility at how much I had shown the crowd.

Decided not to go out for the third round. How could I, only in my underpants? How could I go anywhere now? I looked around the room and there was nothing that I could use to cover myself. How was I going to get back to the dorm?

The first girl came back and looked at me with a smug expression. She had 34-inch boobs, bigger than mine; she was also down to her panties.

The others went on stage and I sat nervously, tried to figure out how was I going to get out of the bar and home dressed this way.

Every girl but one came back topless and a second one had stripped to her panties as well. Missy came back in and my name was called.

I didn't move. No way was I going back on that stage. Shortly after my name was called the second time, Heather and Amanda sauntered into the room.

'Bitches,' I muttered.

'Get up and get out there,' Heather told me. 'You have to go out one more time if you want to win.'

I said, 'Go out there like this? No way. I don't care if I win. How am I going to get out of here without being arrested?'

'You're going on stage,' Amanda said, grabbing my arm. 'C'mon, girl.'

I shrugged her away.

They both grabbed my arms and dragged me to the door and up the stairs. I was trying to cover up but they held my arms down and I saw JoAnne waiting for me with her hands behind her back. She had a nasty smile on her face.

My stomach lurched.

What more could she do to me?

Heather and Amanda led me to the guy with the water hose and I was drenched once more. Immediately my panties began to sag down on my hips and the crowd cheered loudly with fervour when they saw me.

My two friends took me to centre stage and held me there, exposing my little bosoms.

I began to dance, covering my boobs with my hands. My panties were hanging on me, but barely. Once I started dancing, though, the cheers and yells made me feel like I had *the power* once more. I started to give little flashes of my boobs and I really was getting excited. My three dorm friends danced with me. JoAnne was behind me and I felt a touch on my hip. I started to reach down to grab my panties, but I didn't realise that she had cut them with pair of small scissors. The waistband was cut through, my panties slid down. I frantically grabbed for them but I missed as they slid further and further until they were lying on the stage, free from my flesh. I dropped both my hands to cover my pussy and started to turn and run off the stage, but they grabbed me again. My boobs were out in the open as I held both hands over my pussy. Heather and Amanda each grabbed one of my legs and JoAnne pulled both my arms back. I was looking out at the sea of faces in front of me, all the guys out there were cheering and yelling, all those eyes on my crotch. I was so embarrassed; my face was very red and the embarrassment spread all over my body, my white skin going crimson. JoAnne made sure that I couldn't cover my boobs by holding my arms back and Heather and Amanda lifted me by my legs. I knew what they were going to do to me. They lifted me easily. I was the smallest of the four of us by far and weighed only a hundred pounds. When I was lifted up high enough that even the guys in the back could see me,

Heather and Amanda pulled my legs apart. *I wanted to die, I wanted to fall through the stage, and I wanted to be anywhere but there.* They did it slowly, listening to the guys screaming as my legs opened. *I was naked.* I was being held up in the air in front of dozens of guys. JoAnne reached around and cupped my boobs and thumbed my nipples and I felt my labia pull apart. They were showing me – showing *all of me* to the crowd. I turned my head so I would not have to look at the sea of eyes and smiles. Heather and Amanda paraded me to all three sides of the stage, holding my legs open. My nipples were stiff and poking out from the cold water and JoAnne's fingering. My pussy felt wide enough that I was sure people could see all the way inside of me. And yet, as embarrassed as I was, I was also quite excited. I couldn't understand these feelings that I had. I *shouldn't* be excited; I should be mortified, angry, ashamed. I *was* a little, but I was even more excited – sexually aroused. They turned me and held me just like they had for the crowd, for the MC and the guy with the hose and all the other guys on stage. Everyone had a look at me, at my naked body, my pubic hair, *my bush*, my labia and even inside me ... oh, and my boobs.

* * *

It took me a while, but with how turned on I was and with the realisation that nothing I had was a secret any more, I turned to Heather and then Amanda and demanded they put me down. They both grinned at me and lowered my feet to the stage.

I got the three of them beside me. 'Dance with me, bitches.'

Started dancing, this time with abandon, because I knew that there was nothing, not a part of me that was sacred any more. I was unashamed and I danced on that stage with no thought of covering myself. I didn't care what they saw. I turned so my butt was facing the crowd and shook my cheeks. Bent over so they could look at my opened pussy real good. As I did that the MC squatted in front of me and looked up at me. I grinned at him and straightened up. Then I spread my feet apart and tilted my hips forwards. He stared right at my pussy and then looked up at me. He was pleased.

I danced over to each man on that stage and let him look at me, look at any part of me that he wanted to see. I was pretty much out of control. Even without the water that had been sprayed on me I knew that my pussy had to be wet. The music kept playing behind me and I kept dancing. I even bent over and kissed several of the guys in the front row, making sure that my knees were open so they could see what they desired.

I had never been so turned on in my life. I think if I could've gotten away with it, I would've pulled one of those guys on stage and had him screw me in front of everyone. I needed a man that bad. I was determined to get some penis before the night was over.

The MC turned off the music and called for the other girls to come on stage. I stood to one side, naked, with my hands on my hips, smiling at any guy who yelled obscene words at me. The other girls came up and two were pretty shocked to see me standing there naked, three were openly hostile, calling me a slut and a cunt, and one left the stage when she saw me.

Missy walked over to me and gave me a hug. 'You got moxie, girl,' she said.

Then came the voting. The MC held his hand over each girl's head and asked if she was the winner. When he did it to me, I started dancing and strutted from one side of the stage to the other. All my inhibitions were gone, and I felt very free.

I saw Heather, Amanda and JoAnne in front of the stage, applauding and cheering for me. I flipped them the bird. I felt powerful, because I hadn't let them get the best of me, and I had the gumption – the *moxie* – to do what they would not.

* * *

Needless to say, as the only naked girl on stage, I won the $500.

The six remaining girls walked off the stage and I

remembered that I didn't have a stitch to wear. I stopped by one of the big muscular guys and asked him for one of the large T-shirts they were selling with the bar logo. He looked at me, up and down, and then, with a grin, gave me one, free of charge.

Dashed into the room and stripped as much of the water off my skin with my hands as I could. Could hear muttering from the others, calling me a slut, a whore, softly, but loud enough that I could hear. One said something about needing the $500 for rent. I didn't give a crap what they thought.

Slipped the T-shirt over my head and tugged it down. It reached to the middle of my thighs and, even if my nipples and bush showed through it, at least I wasn't *totally* naked any more.

My three devious friends came charging in and hugged me, telling me that they hadn't planned on doing what they did to me, but I seemed to be so 'into it' that they went further. I hugged them back and smiled at them and said, 'What the hell.' I was at peace with the whole night and since the bar was still open for another hour, I said, 'Let's go get some drinks, bitches.'

We barrelled out of the room and into the bar. Got some cheers and walked to the bar and ordered four beers. I paid for the drinks with a $50 bill, from the ten fifties I was given as my prize.

We found a table, and soon we were surrounded by

guys, some really hot and handsome men with bulges under their shirts and between their legs.

I flushed and sat back to enjoy the attention, attention I'd never gotten from men before. Usually guys didn't flock around me because I was plain and didn't have big tits. But now that I had been naked in front of them, I was the Queen of Sexy Flesh and at the moment that felt good. Dirty maybe, but good dirty. I wondered how many guys had seen me tonight, how many went to my school, how many would recognise me on campus. Thinking about it, my head tingled and I felt myself getting wet again.

I was thinking that maybe, just maybe, I might be able to get a hot guy for tonight, or even part of the week.

Maybe I would meet my future husband this way …

Anything seemed possible right then.

My mind started to run through possibilities and I smiled at a hot guy who was smiling at me. I was in control here. I could have whatever, whomever, I wanted.

This *could* be fun, I thought.

A Country Ramble
Penny Birch

The lake looked impossibly tempting. Green water glittered in the bright sunlight, cool and inviting, in sharp contrast to the dry heat of the open downs. All I had to do was make my way down the slope, strip to my bra and knickers and plunge in. There wasn't even anybody about, that I could see, while clumps of bushes and mounds of chalky soil left by the quarrymen who'd originally dug the place out suggested plenty of opportunities for privacy.

Walking back from Whipsnade to Tring had seemed a good idea at the time. The Society lunch had been long and more alcoholic, so I'd needed to clear my head. What I hadn't expected was the glare of sunlight on the chalky soil, or just how hot I would get toiling up the big open slopes of the Chilterns. I didn't need to be back at the pub where my colleagues and I were staying either, not immediately, and the idea of a swim was simply too tempting to resist.

I struck down the slope, now feeling a touch embarrassed by the knowledge that I would shortly be stripping to my underwear in a public place. Yet it was a weekday afternoon and I'd only passed two people all the way from the zoo, both solitary, middle-aged walkers. Nobody was likely to see, and if they didn't they were unlikely to be offended. That was all very well, but I've always found going naked or even near naked both embarrassing and exciting, and now was no exception.

As I descended, the air grew stiller, and hotter, until the sweat was trickling down my face. I needed to get into the water, badly, only to reach the edge of the lake and discover that what I'd thought was dry chalk was in fact mud, or more accurately a sort of thick greyish-white slurry left by the retreating water during the unusually dry spring. My shoes would be ruined within a few steps, and the open water was a good fifty yards away, which meant I'd have to strip off somewhere private and make a dash for the lake. It was a pleasantly naughty thought, adding to my gradually building arousal and tempting me to do it properly and go naked. In any case, my colleagues and I had been sharing the washing, and if my underwear came into contact with the mud it was going to take a lot of explaining.

If there's one thing better than going naked on purpose it's feeling you have no choice in the matter. I chose a quiet spot among clumps of wild rose at one end of the old quarry, well out of sight, and began to strip off. Just shedding my blouse was a pleasure, my first even faintly erotic act in days. Normally I'd masturbate most nights, but I was in a double room, while seminars on ecological genetics don't leave much scope for naughty thoughts.

My skirt followed my blouse, then my bra, my shoes, my tights and finally my panties. I was naked, deliciously naked, bare to the world in the hot sun, with my nipples already erect and my pussy in need of a stroke. That was going to have to wait until I was absolutely sure of my privacy, although I'd already decided to do it, because stripping off for a swim is one thing, but playing with yourself in public is quite another.

I hid my bag in the depths of a wild rose bush, just in case, then made my way back to the edge of the mud. Now I could be seen from the downs, stark naked, which gave a deliciously naughty thrill for all that there was nobody in sight. Nevertheless, there was every chance there would be, so I didn't waste any time, stepping forwards with one hand over my boobs and the other on top of my pussy – a fairly silly thing to do, but it felt right.

The mud was deliciously cool, and from the moment I felt my toes squash into it I knew I'd have to go in

142

properly, kneeling at the very least. It was also deep, and got quickly thicker so that I was soon up to my ankles and having trouble keeping my balance. When I slipped I just let go, falling back to sit my bottom squarely into the cold, sticky muck. It felt glorious, so good I took a moment just to wriggle myself into the mess, deliberately enjoying the disgusting sensation of having the thick, grey ooze squeeze up between my cheeks and over my pussy.

That wasn't enough. A glance at the downs showed that I was still alone, so I took two big handfuls of mud and squashed them over my boobs, rubbing it in and playing with my nipples through the cool slime. Now I was thoroughly soiled, and it would have been lovely to go to work on my filthy, slippery cunt then and there, masturbating in the thick grey mud until I came. Unfortunately that was just too risky, so I contented myself with crawling a little way on my hands and knees, imagining how I'd look with my filthy boobs swinging under my chest and my badly soiled bottom wobbling behind me, perhaps with the pink of my slit and bum hole showing behind.

I'd only gone a little way before I lost my nerve and scrabbled to my feet to run the rest of the way, or at least try to run, because by the time I reached the water's edge I was sinking halfway up my calves with every step. That meant I was in trouble, because there was no obvious way of getting back to my clothes without getting my legs filthy, while the chances of falling over by accident had to be pretty high. There would nothing for it but to wait, naked, until the chalky mud had dried and I could brush it off.

That's just the sort of situation I love, erotic and help-less, with a touch of the ridiculous to bring out my love of humiliation. As I plunged into the cool water, which was every bit as welcome as I'd anticipated, I was imag-ining how it would be, trying to resist playing with myself as I waited, nude and embarrassed, before finally giving in to my dirty needs and bringing myself off under my fingers.

I swam out towards the middle of the lake, quickly reaching the deep, green water I'd admired from the downs. A brief period of treading water and I'd got the mud off, leaving me bare and pink. Somebody was now visible, another lone walker making his way across the hillside, and I wondered if he'd see me and, if he did, whether he'd realise I was naked. He was so far off it was hard to be sure, and he didn't give any sign of atten-tion, but I found myself striking out for a cluster of little islands where the quarrymen had left mounds of chalk.

Once among them I was invisible, as each rose several feet from the water and was thickly grown with bushes. It was also shallower, and in places the low water level had left small, flat areas of fresh, pale mud, areas completely invisible from the shore. I stood up, my legs sinking deep into the bottom, tried to wade and promptly lost my balance, falling face forwards into the mess.

I'd gone over at least half on purpose before, but this was a genuine accident and I'd soiled my belly and breasts, even splashed my face. Once again I was dirty, and this time there was no holding back. I struggled to my hands and knees, crawled forwards a little way and turned myself over, deliberately sitting my bottom down in the mud. It was far deeper than before, not only squashing up between my cheeks to soil my anus and cunt, but engulfing me to the hips, so that I was sitting in a small crater of thick grey slime.

My hands went to my chest, slapping two heavy handfuls of goo over my breasts and rubbing it in as before. I was squirming my bottom in the filth as I pulled at my nipples, lost in my dirty behaviour and wondering what else I could do to make the state I was in worse still. My face had to go in, there was no question about it, even if it left me unable to see while I brought myself off. I knew I was safe, and yet I'd still feel that much more vulnerable.

Kneeling forwards once more, with my bottom stuck provocatively high behind me and my face just inches from the surface of the mud, I took myself by the hair, as if somebody else was about to push my face in the mud as a punishment, or to humiliate me, waited a moment to

145

savour my helplessness and disgust, then pushed sharply down. My face went into the mud with a wet, squashy sound, followed by a sucking noise as I pulled free, only to repeat the motion. This time I kept my mouth open, filling it with foul grey muck. It tasted horrible, but that was part of the fun, and of the fantasy building in my head as I rocked back to sit my bottom in the filth once more and let my fingers find my eager, greedy cunt.

I imagined how it would be, with some random man taking me down to the lake for a punishment. First he'd make me strip in front of him, stark naked. Next he'd put me across his knee and spank me, and perhaps make me kiss his balls or take his cock in my mouth, just to reinforce his authority over me. Then it would be down to the lake and into the mud, pushed over to get me dirty, handfuls of filth plastered over my boobs and into my hair, between my legs too. I'd be begging him to spare my face, but of course he wouldn't, taking me firmly by the hair and forcing my head into the deepest, most revolting patch of mud he could find. The second time I went down I'd get caught with my mouth open, but still he'd show no mercy. Even as I struggled to spit out the filthy mess clogging my throat, he'd stick his cock in my mouth, forcing me to swallow, then to suck him until he was fully erect.

My fingers were working busily in the slimy mud-filled slit of my cunt, with my free hand clutching at my filthy breasts. I was already on the edge of orgasm and, as I started to come, I tipped myself forwards once more, my knees set wide and my bottom thrust high and open. My face went back in the filth, my mouth wide to take in as much as I possibly could, even as I reached back between my bottom cheeks to find the slimy little ring of my anus. I pushed a finger up my bottom, and a second, deliberately spreading my slippery hole as I imagined the climax of my punishment.

I'd know I was going to be used, and that there was no escape, but as he pulled his cock from my mouth to leave me spitting filth I'd be begging him to spare my cunt. He'd agree and, as he got behind me and forced me back down into a crawling position with my face held in the filth, I'd know exactly where his cock was going, up my dirty bottom hole to give me a good, hard buggering before he spunked up in my rectum. On that thought I came.

* * *

It took quite a while to wash all the mud off, especially to get it out of my hair, and once I was completely clean I treated myself to a long leisurely swim, no longer aroused but simply enjoying the freedom of being alone and naked. One or two people passed by on the downs, but for most of the time I was hidden from view among the islands at the far end of the lake from where I'd got in. Eventually, I began to get cold and decided it was time to come out, using an ancient shoe and a piece of plastic to allow me to get back to my clothes without getting plastered with mud, only to discover that I had no clothes to get back to.

At first I thought I'd made a mistake, as one clump of wild rose looks much like the next, but my bag was still where I'd hidden it. Somebody had taken my clothes, somebody who was presumably still nearby, enjoying my nakedness and enjoying my confusion. I glanced around, frightened but also determined and not wanting to show my vulnerability. Nobody was visible and there was no hint that anybody was about at all, but I was sure they'd be watching and my hands had gone to cover my breasts and sex once more.

'OK,' I shouted. 'A joke's a joke. You can give me back my clothes now.'

There was no answer, and I hadn't really expected there to be. Peeping Toms don't work that way, but I knew it was sensible to put on a bold front. I raised my arms, showing off my naked body and making a slow turn, hoping to shame him into letting me out of my predicament.

'There you are,' I called. 'Now you've seen me naked. That's what you want, isn't it? Now throw my clothes out and go away.'

Still there was no answer, and I found myself biting my lip. There was no way of covering myself, but if the peeping Tom was still about, and he almost had to be, then the last thing I wanted to do was go somewhere I couldn't be seen. My best option was to climb the slope back up to the open downs, naked, exposed to anybody and everybody who happened to be passing, but relatively safe. I made one last appeal.

'Please?' I said, trying to keep the choking note out of my voice. 'This isn't fair!'

There was no response and I started off alongside the lake, clutching my bag over my pussy and seething at the thought of the man who was probably still watching me, both for what he'd done and for what he was making me do, but mainly for the pleasure I knew he'd be taking not only in my nudity but in my discomfort. Some of that pleasure would be no more than mischief, but the situation could hardly fail to turn him on and it was all too easy to imagine his eyes fixed on my bare, wobbling bottom as I retreated, quite possibly while he used my stolen panties to rub at his cock.

I quickened my pace at the thought and reached the ancient fence that marked the boundary of the quarry and quickly climbed over. The only sensible thing to do was to find the nearest house, explain the situation to the occupants and pray they were sympathetic. I hurried on, blushing hot at the thought of what I'd have to do, but with no choice. My embarrassment was increasing with every step, and I wasn't even sure which was worse, being caught running around in the nude or having to knock on somebody's door in the same sorry state.

Something red caught my eye among the trees in the direction I'd been going in the first place: the corner of a lorry trailer. I turned towards it without hesitation, now at a run and thinking of bits of old canvas or sacking, anything to cover my naked body before I met somebody. There was a fence by the trees but I was over it in a moment, only to discover a second one, much higher, that closed off a small trailer park. For one awful moment I thought I was going to end up exhibiting myself naked in front of half a dozen lorry drivers on the far side of a fence I couldn't cross, but some blessed vandal had hacked a hole in the wire and I was able to squeeze through.

The lorry park seemed to be deserted, with the big red rig and four others parked on open dusty concrete. At the far side was a gate, and by it a sort of booth, with the door half open and hanging from a nail on the back an ancient scruffy overcoat. The most beautiful of gowns could not have been more welcome and I was skipping across the hot concrete on the instant, very much aware that any drivers in the cabs would be getting a prime view of my little streak but determined to get to that coat if it meant exhibiting myself to every trucker in the country.

I reached the door, threw it open, grabbed the coat and stopped, eye to eye with a man in blue overalls seated inside the booth, his round red face frozen in astonishment, his pop eyes fixed on my naked body, one hand stopped in the act of turning a page of the magazine he was reading. The magazine was full of naked young women in vulgar poses, while in his other hand he held a large reddish cock, half stiff with excitement. I felt it was up to me to open the conversation, but not until I was covered up, and he spoke as I was struggling into the coat.

'Oi, that's my coat!'

'Sorry,' I apologised, 'but I was naked. Somebody stole my clothes, down by the lake.'

He nodded, his eyes still lingering on me and his face now showing a trace of disappointment, although he at least had the decency to put his cock away. I was blushing furiously and conscious of a strong need to explain my behaviour.

'I was swimming,' I told him. 'It's such a hot day. Look, um … I don't suppose you could help me out? I'm staying in Tring, if you wouldn't mind giving me a lift?'

He pondered my suggestion for a moment before replying. 'I've got to stay here, I have.'

'Yes, but it wouldn't take five minutes.'

'I have to keep an eye on the trailers. I can't leave until the end of my shift.'

'When's that?'

'Midnight.'

'Oh. Couldn't you lock up for a while and come back? I'd be ever so grateful.'

Too late I realised the implications of what I'd said, at least to a man like him, a man who masturbated over dirty magazines.

His mouth had twitched up into a nasty little grin. 'How grateful?' he asked.

'I didn't mean it like that,' I said hastily. 'Please, just be nice?'

'I'll be nice if you're nice.'

I hid a sigh. There was no escaping his logic. He'd already seen me naked, which made me wonder if I could get what I needed without further sacrifice.

'Look,' I told him, 'how about if I take the coat off and you … you can finish what you were doing?'

A small, fat tongue flicked out to moisten his lips. 'Yeah, all right.'

I let the coat slip from my shoulders and hung it back on the peg, leaving myself naked once more, only full of chagrin rather than embarrassment. After an appraising glance of my body, he unzipped his fly to pull out his cock and balls once more. He was quite big, with a thick reddish-brown cock resting on a bulging scrotum, and already half hard. I found myself swallowing and trying to fight down my instinctive, dirty reaction, promising that just for once I'd keep what little dignity remained to me.

'Come on then,' he urged as he began to pull at his cock, 'give us a bit of a show, you know, like the girls in the mags.'

He'd jerked his thumb at the magazine he'd been reading as he spoke, indicating the pictures of girls on the page he'd been looking at. They were all naked or in scraps of tarty clothing, and in rude poses, the least vulgar of which showed a buxom blonde holding her breasts up. I did my best to imitate the pose, my blushes growing hotter and my sense of humiliation stronger as I cupped my breasts for him.

'Nice,' he drawled, 'only, don't take this the wrong way or nothing, but you ain't got too much up top. I bet you've got a nice round bum though.'

I made a face and gave what I hoped was a disapproving tut, but turned around to show him my bottom. He immediately began to pull harder on his cock, which was now almost fully erect. I knew what he'd want and had already arched my back, showing off as blatantly as any of the girls in the magazine.

'Oh, yeah,' he sighed, 'you do have a nice bum, a very nice bum. Come on, stick it out a little bit more. Show us your brown eye. Show us your cunt.'

This time I made no effort to hide my answering sigh, but it was as much in despair for my own reaction as for his dirty behaviour. I love being treated like that, I can't help it, and, as I pushed out my bottom into a yet ruder position and swung round a little to let him get a full show of my rear view, I was fighting the urge to let go completely.

'Fuck me but you're lovely,' he groaned, now hammering at his fully erect penis, 'fucking gorgeous, so hairy, and the way your slit shows, and your little pink arsehole, so soft. I bet you've had a man or two up that, ain't you?'

I broke. 'Go on, just do it, you dirty bastard. Bugger me!'

He didn't need telling twice. I was pushed forwards even as he got up from his chair, forced to brace myself against the wall with my bottom thrust out, my cheeks well spread and my anus stretched wide between. I stuck a finger in my mouth, meaning to get myself ready, but he simply spat, full between my cheeks, and pushed the fat, bloated head of his cock to my hole, rubbing in the phlegm to help open me up even as I pushed out to accept him.

It hurt, and I was grunting and panting as he jammed himself up me, but I wanted it and he was in no mood to slow down, calling me a bitch and a whore as he forced his erection gradually in my bottom hole. I was rubbing myself before he'd even got right in, masturbating as he buggered me with his balls slapping against my busy fingers. He began to slap my bottom too, adding spanking to the list of humiliations inflicted on me, and that was just too much. I came, in a long tight orgasm, with my bum hole squeezing on his intruding cock shaft, even as he called me a filthy little bitch one last time and shot his load, with the contractions of my anal ring milking him into my rectum.

He was very nice about it afterwards. One of the trailers turned out to be full of cheap dresses, made in Laos, and, as I slipped into one, I couldn't help but reflect that if I'd only had the sense to try the doors I'd have been spared a buggering, or to be honest, that I'd have missed out on one of the nicest, dirtiest buggerings of my life. He hadn't even told me his name, and I hadn't given him mine, but I only realised as I walked away down the lane and it seemed silly to turn back.

The unexpected treat hadn't made my feelings for the man who'd stolen my clothes any less bitter, while I was unpleasantly aware that he might still be about. The lane soon joined a small road, which I realised ran along the woods at the back of the quarry, and I was relieved to see a group of three women with gloves on and holding black sacks, which they were filling with cans, crisp packets and other rubbish. Only as I got close did an embarrassing possibility occur to me, but I had to ask and approached the nearest, an elderly virago in expensive-looking tweeds.

'Excuse me. I don't suppose you were clearing up by the old quarry earlier on? Only I've misplaced some clothes.'

The look she gave me was pure contempt, but she had reached into her bag to extract a piece of limp, badly soiled cotton which had once been white, my knickers.

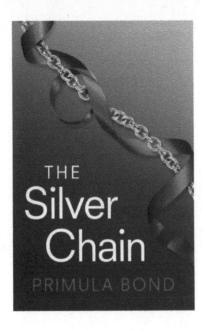

THE SILVER CHAIN – PRIMULA BOND

Good things come to those who wait…

After a chance meeting one evening, mysterious entrepreneur Gustav Levi and photographer Serena Folkes agree to a very special contract.

Gustav will launch Serena's photographic career at his gallery, but only if Serena agrees to become his companion.

To mark their agreement, Gustav gives Serena a bracelet and silver chain which binds them physically and symbolically. A sign that Serena is under Gustav's power.

As their passionate relationship intensifies, the silver chain pulls them closer together. But will Gustav's past tear them apart?

A passionate, unforgettable erotic romance for fans of *50 Shades of Grey* and Sylvia Day's *Crossfire Trilogy*.

GAME – JUSTINE ELYOT

The stakes are high, the game is on.

In this sequel to Justine Elyot's bestselling *On Demand*, Sophie discovers a whole new world of daring sexual exploits.

Sophie's sexual tastes have always been a bit on the wild side – something her boyfriend Lloyd has always loved about her.

But Sophie gives Lloyd every part of her body except her heart. To win all of her, Lloyd challenges Sophie to live out her secret fantasies.

As the game intensifies, she experiments with all kinds of kinks and fetishes in a bid to understand what she really wants. But Lloyd feature in her final decision? Or will the ultimate risk he takes drive her away from him?

Find out more at www.mischiefbooks.com

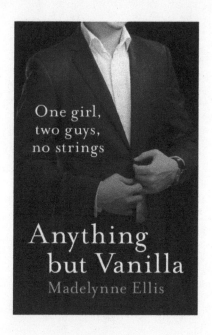

ANYTHING BUT VANILLA
MADELYNNE ELLIS

One girl, two guys, no strings.

Kara North is on the run. Fleeing from her controlling fiancé and a wedding she never wanted, she accepts the chance offer of refuge on Liddell Island, where she soon catches the eye of the island's owner, erotic photographer Ric Liddell.

But pleasure comes in more than one flavour when Zachary Blackwater, the charming ice-cream vendor also takes an interest, and wants more than just a tumble in the surf.

When Kara learns that the two men have been unlikely lovers for years, she becomes obsessed with the idea of a threesome.

Soon Kara is wondering how she ever considered committing herself to just one man.

Find out more at www.mischiefbooks.com